Oops
My Dreams

Oops
My Dreams

For People Who Feel That
Dreams Can Come True

Ashish Kumar Jha

PARTRIDGE
A Penguin Random House Company

ISBN:	Hardcover	978-1-4828-4173-2
	Softcover	978-1-4828-4174-9
	eBook	978-1-4828-4172-5

Print information available on the last page.

To order additional copies of this book, contact
Partridge India
000 800 10062 62
orders.india@partridgepublishing.com

www.partridgepublishing.com/india

Contents

Acknowledgements

It was not at all easy to write this book but thanks to my parents, wife, sister, and brother-in-law for instilling the confidence in me that I can write and for being with me through thick and thin. I would like to thank my friends for suggesting to read good books that helped me to understand what writing is all about. I would like to take this opportunity to thank all of those people who have helped me in their own capacity which eventually helped me to write and put my ideas in this book.

Preface

No one knew how it happened but the world's most revered country turned into such a weak nation that no one would have imagined in the wildest of dreams that this would happen one day. Brothers have become foe, old people are humiliated everyday of their lives, women are scared whether they are safe in their own motherland or not and the new born can see no future ahead. Corruption, crime, illiteracy, unemployment, lacuna in law and order system and poor security mechanisms are making the country crumble in each passing day. The nation has become a soft target by the terrorists and the people are not safe within the country. Still there are dreamers who say that the country shall come out of all evils and there shall be a beautiful morning that each and every AlphaLandite shall witness one day. Each and every AlphaLandite shall work for the betterment of the nation and shall make the nation so strong and prosperous that the world have never witnessed before. This book is the epitome of the dreams of the common man who feels that dreams do come true.

Dreams

When its dark everywhere and there is no light
When there is nothing that goes right
When you feel there is no delight
Then there is still something that works as said by wise
    and bright
It's dreams, it's dreams that keep the hopes alive and it
    can be your might

When you find everywhere corruption
When you see that there is only vandalism
When you lose your faith in the system
When you see there is no other option
Then there are still dreams that can give solution

When you find only crime, crime, and crime
When lots of evil deeds happen Clandestine
When women and children are killed for a dime
When common man has to follow countless lines
Then there are only dreams that say everything
    shall be fine

When old people and innocents fear of being battered
When they feel they are not accoutred
When female feticide is on high and is every day
    encountered
When no one is with you when you feel shattered
Then there are dreams that make you strong and you
    are not afraid

Chapter One

Arrival at AlphaLand

It was two in the afternoon. I had just finished my lunch and I was sitting in the balcony. It was heavily raining, the roads were completely deserted and even the dogs on the street were searching for places to hide. Mom had already given a pre-alert for 6:00 p.m. class. Oh, gosh, again the same class, same boring teacher, same classmates, no beautiful girls, and on the top of it the boring math subject and that, too, on this rainy day. Please someone kill these classes. I don't want to attend them.

I was feeling sleepy as the food that I had for lunch was quite delicious which my mom very well knows how to prepare as much as she knows how to make me remind of those stuff which I don't want to do. Moms are after all moms, no arguments.

No sooner, sitting idle, I fell asleep and all of a sudden I was in a different world. Oh, where the hell am I? *Aaah!* Tall buildings, *oooh!* skyscrapers, wider roads, greenery everywhere, beautiful houses and offices, amazing malls, eye-catching food joints, amazing vehicles, cleanliness everywhere, no beggars, and many more which shall be witnessed going forward as saying in few words would be like praising a beautiful lady without any words, I mean, doing injustice.

I saw a lovely cafeteria and I had a curiosity to see it so without wasting much time, I sneaked inside it. Oh, it was so huge, tall ceilings, big aisles, it was an awesome restaurant. Just I was wondering where to sit, I saw a beautiful lady who was sitting alone with a cup of coffee, I guess. She must be waiting for someone like me and with this thought I proceeded towards her.

I approached her and very politely I asked whether she would allow me to share the table with her. After thinking for a few moments she agreed. She was very beautiful; someone whom you would like to see again and again and still your desire to see her shall not die. I asked her for her name and with a lovely husky voice she replied. I made myself feel comfortable and went to get my coffee. Oh, yeah, there were so many varieties of coffee I just could not understand which one to pick up so I pointed my finger to the most eye-catching one. I guess I made myself comfortable with hot chocolatae gubaoae latteae. The coffee was simply amazing! Something like I never had before. Oops, sorry, Mom, but I have to admit it, you can't be good at everything.

She asked me from where I came from. I told her I came from AlphaLand, one of the most prominent countries in the world map for all the reasons, you have to just name it. Thus, my story with the beautiful young lady begins.

'You are from AlphaLand? Are you kidding?'

'Listen, Jeena, what is so funny if I am from AlphaLand? It may not be as beautiful as your country but still it's a very important nation and I am proud of it.'

"Saandip, if you are from AlphaLand then why don't you look like us. Why are you so amazed by looking at this place? Why are you not looking comfortable here? Why it is obvious on your face that you are surprised by looking at this place as if you have come in to some alien world? Buddy, for your information, the country where are you are right now is AlphaLand and I guess there is only one AlphaLand in the world so you need to correct yourself.'

'Look, Jeena, I know you are damn gorgeous but sometimes pretty girls make mistake. Pretty girls are always out of their brains.' *Oops!* I can't say this to her. 'Jeena, I think you should correct yourself, this country shall be something else. I guess yesterday you may have seen AlphaLand in some movies so it may be still at the back of your mind and that is the reason by mistake you are saying your country's name is AlphaLand. The men in AlphaLand are very handsome so you may have likened this place for something like that.'

'What the hell? You want to say I have forgotten the name of my country? Correct yourself, this place is AlphaLand and I belong to this great nation.'

'But how is it possible? I belong to AlphaLand and it does not look like this.'

'Saandip, I guess you are little tired, why don't you finish your coffee you shall feel bit better.'

'Very funny.'

'When you are done with your coffee then I would like to show you this great country. I would like to show you how beautiful this nation is.'

'I am done, let's go and see your version of AlphaLand and as claimed by you, the real AlphaLand.'

'It's not funny, can we go now?'

'As I said, I am curious to see, so let's go.'

'Okay then, let's go.'

'Sure.'

'Can I call you Sands?'

'What?'

'The shorter form of your name.'

'Let me think.'

'I guess you didn't like it. I shall call you Saandip only?'

'Hey, hey, hello, madam, you have been calling me Saandip. It's not Saandip, it's Sandeep, okay?'

'Ohh, I am sorry I will call you Sandeep.'

'Well, on one condition you can call me Sands.'

'What condition?'

'If you allow me to call you Jeans.'

'What Jeans? Am I some trousers or pants, what?'

'Jeena is a very good name but Jeans is the shorter form of that.'

'What shorter form? The number of alphabets in both the names are same.'

'Well, I just wanted to give you some name from my end. Hope you don't mind it.'

'Okay, then you call me Jeans and I shall call you Sands. Fine.'

'Yuppieee!'

Chapter Two

First Outing in AlphaLand

'Oye! What's that? Why is that man so happy?'

'Well, I don't know. Let's go and find it out.'

'Sure.'

'Hey, hi mate, what's your name?'

'Hi, I am Robes. What's your name?'

'I am Jeena and he is Sandeep. He is our guest at AlphaLand.'

'Hi, 'Saandip it's nice to meet you and welcome to AlphaLand. Jeena nice to meet you too, how are you doing?'

'Well, I am good. How are you doing, Robes?'

'Well, I am good, Jeena. Just wanted to know, have we met earlier or are we meeting for the first time?'

'No, I don't think we have met earlier. We were just passing by and I was showing him our beautiful country and in between we saw you very happy. You were jumping with joy so we became curious and wanted to know the reason of your happiness. If it is fine with you, may we know why you are so happy?'

'Ohh, not at all why should I mind telling you why I am so happy today. It's a great day for me today. It's just like I am on seventh heaven, I just got the job that I desired. I have been dreaming to get this job since my school days!'

'What job did you get?'

'Are you seeing this big building?'

'Yes, it is Mildionae.'

'Yes, very true, Mildionae, the biggest and most desired working place of this country. Look at its splendour, look at the emblem, look at the people who are working here they look so proud and look at the uniforms these people are wearing it's simply shining on their body. These guys are our saviours and our heroes. We sleep safely at our homes, we roam safely on the streets, we eat the delicious stuffs at restaurants, we visit so many places throughout the length and breadth of the country and we live the way we want to only because these people are there protecting us all days and nights without break throughout the year. We are proud of our heroes the AlphaLand national guards.

'You are so right, Robes.'

'Since childhood I have been watching this building, the headquarters of the AlphaLand national guards and from then only I had the dream to work here one day. Today, I got this opportunity. Today, my dream has come true and that's why I am so happy. This is a great day of my life!'

'Hey, congrats, buddy, it's really great news!'

'Thanks, guys.'

'Robes, you enjoy your great moment we shall now take a leave from you. Hope to see you again.'

'Thanks, guys, and any problems do call me, from now onwards I am also one of your protectors. Hey, 'Saandip, you got to see this great nation. Our country is simply heaven on earth.'

'Thanks, Robes.'

'Okay, guys, take care.'

'You too, Robes, take good care of yourself.'

'Hey, Jeans, he looked so happy. I guess it's like a dream job for people in this country.'

'Yeah, Sands, it's a dream job for people in AlphaLand. It's an honour to serve the people and the nation.'

'He may have had heavy contacts otherwise it would have been difficult for him to get this job. I mean getting a government job is quite difficult. It is easier to walk on water than finding a government job. Without contacts one cannot even imagine it.'

'What makes you say that?'

'There are so many things like seats scarcity, reservations, recommendations and the list goes on and on and on. Once the person gets the job then that person gets an opportunity to play with gold mine and in a very few years that person can become a millionaire.'

'What the hell are you saying? No recommendations and contacts can work. Only merit works in AlphaLand and one gets a job on his or her own merit.'

'Jeans, I am from AlphaLand and I know what happens there.'

'Ohh, really, Sands?'

'Yes.'

'What do you know? Sands. Sands.'

#####

'Dad, I guess this time I am sure that I will make it. I mean everything right from the written exam to the final interview has gone well.'

'Great, son.'

'This is my last chance, Dad, and I don't want to miss it. Since childhood it has been my dream to work as a policeman and serve my country and my countrymen. I am going to fulfil it this time.'

'Don't worry, son, my heart says that this time you will make it.'

'Thanks, Dad.'

'Hey, your mom has made your favourite dish.'

'Wow! That's great! Hey, Mom, thanks for this, it has been ages since I had it.'

'Now you have become so big that you will say thanks to your mom?'

'Ohh, I didn't mean that, Mom. What I meant was it's really great to have my favourite dish today.'

'Eat your food now.'

'Sure, Mom.'

'So how is the food?'

'Dad, it's awesome as always.'

'Really awesome. Laxmae, I guess you still have the old charm left in you in abundance.'

'Now don't embarrass me in front of Sudipae.'

'Mom, Dad is flirting with you.'

'Will you stop applying your mind in all these kind of things and eat your food?'

'I was just saying.'

'Sudipae.'

'Okay fine, Mom, I am having my food.'

'After food take proper rest, son. Tomorrow is a big day for you.'

'Sure, Dad.'

'Okay, then I am done with my food so I will take a leave now. I am going to the study room. I have not sat for the entire day today so I'm feeling a little uncomfortable.'

'I know how you must be feeling today, Dad. I guess study is your second wife.'

'Sudipae.'

'Aah, Mom, I am also done with my dinner so I will go to bed. Goodnight, Dad. Goodnight, Mom.'

'Goodnight, son.'

'Sudipae doesn't even know what he speaks about.'

'Oh come on, Laxmae, he is a kid.'

'Don't defend him so much it shall spoil him.'

'Okay, I am getting late, goodnight.

'I hope you will come for sleep on time.'

'Why are you asking that?'

'Goodnight.'

'Sometimes you confuse me, Laxmae.'

'Don't be late.'

'Okay.'

*****

'Good morning, Dad. Good morning, Mom.'

'Hey, good morning, son, hope you had a sound sleep.'

'Yes, Dad, but I was little bit nervous too.'

'Ah, don't get so worried, everything shall be fine.'

'Dad, can I see the newspapers?'

'But these newspapers are of yesterday. Today's papers are yet to be delivered.'

'Dad, it's almost nine in the morning and still the newspapers have not been delivered.'

'Hmmm.'

'It never happens to be so late.'

'You are right, it never happens to be so late, son.'

'Today is an important day for me and the newspapers fellow has not yet delivered the papers. I have to see my results.'

'Cool down, boy. The newspapers will come.'

'When?'

'Okay, I have to go outside. I will come back in sometime.'

'Dad, if you find the newspapers then please bring them for me.'

'Okay.'

'Mom, when will the newspapers come?'

'Why don't you take a bath and get ready? The newspapers may come by that time.'

'Where did Dad go?'

'I don't know, he didn't say anything to me.'

'Okay, I am going to get ready. If the papers come then please let me know.'

'Sure.'

*****

'Laxmae! Laxmae!'

'What?'

'Where is he?'

'He has gone to take a bath.'

'Good, so is everything ready?'

'Yes, but what about the sweets?'

'Here they are.'

'Great! So let's put everything properly in the plates.'

'Laxmae, it has been ages since I had this type of breakfast.'

'Why, don't I serve you proper breakfast daily?'

'No, no, I am not saying that. What I meant is this breakfast is with great celebrations, it's special.'

'Yeah, very true. Sudipae's dream has come true. My son is going to be a big man, it's celebration time!'

'But Laxmae, you were always strict to him.'

'Yes, I know, but it was for his good only.'

'Hmmm.'

'It shall be a big surprise for him. He is looking for the newspapers to see the results and we are hiding the papers from him. How long are we going to hide the good news from him? I think we should now tell him.'

'It's a matter of a few minutes and we shall tell him. This celebration can't be plain and simple, there has to be some surprise and spice, the situation demands it. Our son is going to be a big man now, his dream has come true then how can we keep the celebrations simple?'

'You have become old but your childlike behaviour is still alive.'

'Haaaaaa!'

'I hope everything is properly set now.'

'Just check whether he is ready or not. Ask him to come fast if he is ready.'

'Okay, let me check first.'

'Sure.'

******

'Sudipae, are you ready? Dad has come back and he is asking for you.'

'Mom, I am almost through. Has the newspapers fellow delivered the papers?'

'No, son, not yet.'

'I will not spare that fellow.'

'Okay, you first come out of the bathroom and get ready.'

'Mom, has Dad brought the newspapers?'

'No, I guess the newspapers were sold out.'

'When will I be able to see my result?'

'First, will you get ready and come down. Your dad is waiting for you.'

'Yeah, I am coming.'

'Come fast.'

'Okay.'

*****

'Where is Sudipae?'

'He is coming.'

'Let's sit there.'

'Yeah.'

'I hope he will enjoy the celebration.'

'I hope so.'

'Great!'

'Hi, Dad. Hi, Mom.'

'So, son, are you ready?'

'Yes.'

'So shall we go for breakfast then?'

'But this newspaper fellow has not given papers till now.'

'Ah, true. I don't know what happened to him today.'

'Let's discuss these things over at the breakfast table.'

'Sure, Laxmae.'

'Oh, what is this, Mom?'

'What?'

'So many dishes and sweets for breakfast! Is there anything special today?'

'Yes, son. It's a very special day today!'

'What's the occasion, Dad?'

'First of all, have the sweets.'

'Why?'

'Sudipae we will let you know but come have sweets from my hands first.'

'What's the occasion, Mom?'

'How are the sweets?'

'It's nice but can you tell me the occasion?'

'Sudipae, will you now have the sweets from my hand as well.'

'I am confused.'

'Sweets, please.'

'Okay, Dad.'

'Good.'

'Now can someone tell me the reason?'

'First of all, congratulations to you, son.'

'For what?'

'You have been selected, Sudipae. You got fortieth rank!

'I have been selected? But how do you know that, Dad?'

'We have seen the results in the papers!'

'Which papers?'

'Newspapers, son.'

'But they have not been delivered as yet.'

'The newspapers were delivered, son.'

'What?'

'We saw the results and pretended as if the papers have not been delivered.'

'Oh my goodness!'

'We wanted to give you a surprise, son.'

'Dad, this is not fair!'

'I know, son, but this is a great day and how can we let it go plain and simple without any surprises?'

'This is so wrong, Dad.'

'We are sorry, son.'

'Mom, you too were involved in this?'

'Sorry, son.'

'Let me hold my breath first. It's really tough to believe that I got selected.'

'Yes, son, you did it!'

'At last!'

'You are a champion my son!'

'I did it! I did it! I did it!

'Yes, son, you did it!'

'Can I see the results?'

'Why, you don't believe us?'

'No, it's not that. I just want to see once. I mean I want to feel it.'

'Sure, son, the papers are lying near the table but first have your breakfast.'

'One moment, Mom. I shall be back in a few seconds. *Woohha!* I have done it!'

'Sudipae!'

'Laxmae, let him go and see the results. He can't be stopped now, he is in his own world right now.'

'I love you, Dad and Mom! You are the best in the world!'

'Sudipae, you are the best son in the world.'

'Thanks, Mom. Thanks, Dad. Thanks for being with me always.'

'We are always with you, son.'

'*Woohha! Woohha!* My name is written in bold letters!'

'Yes, son, it's written in bold letters.'

'I am in seventh heaven today! This is the best day of my life!'

'Sudipae, all your favourite dishes are made so let's celebrate on the breakfast table.'

'Coming, Dad.'

'We are proud of you, son.'

'Dad, let's go to Lae Palae for dinner tonight.'

'Good idea, son.'

'But we should not be late while coming home as tomorrow you have to go for the documents submission.'

'Of course, Mom.'

'Son, as now you have got selected to a very good job so your future is secured and we are happy.'

'Thanks, Mom.'

'Laxmae, I just can't believe my ears, you are talking to Sudipae like this.'

'What?'

'It's a surprise for me also, Dad. Mom has never talked to me like this. She has always been strict to me.'

'It was for your betterment.'

'I agree to this, Sudipae. Had she not been strict with you, then you would have never achieved what you got today. I was always busy with my work and most of the time she was with you. She ensured that you are imparted with good values, culture, and academics. Today, all this is because of her dedication and hard work.'

'I love you, Mom.'

'I love you too, my sunny.'

'Okay, guys, I am getting late for my office, so I better make a move now. Be ready in the evening for the Lae Palae dinner.'

'Sure, Dad.'

'Bye, guys!'

'Bye, Dad!'

*****

'Good morning, sir, my name is Sudipae.'

'So?'

'I got the fortieth rank all over AlphaLand in the police service competition.'

'So?'

'I came to submit my documents.'

'What documents?'

'Sir, in yesterday's papers it was mentioned to submit the documents related to mark sheets, date of birth, and graduation certificates within ten days' time.

'Tell me your name.'

'Sir, my name is Sudipae.'

'Sudipae . . . Sudipae . . . but your name is not here in the final list.'

'No, sir, it must be there.'

'You know better or I know. I am saying once again and listen carefully that your name is not here in the final list.'

'How it is possible? My name was there in bold letters in the list which was published in yesterday's newspapers. Please check that list.'

'Haaaaaa!'

'What happened?'

'I think you have not read today's papers.'

'Today's papers?'

'We have published a revised list. By mistake we have published a wrong list yesterday.'

'Is this some joke? I called up here and I was told I got the fortieth rank and I am selected. Please check once again, my name has to be there.'

'I don't know with whom you have talked and what that person has told you.'

'I had a word with Mr Sujelikae.'

'See, Mr Sujelikae is on leave and he is expected after fifteen days.'

'But how can that happen?'

'Oh, I am so sorry he has not taken your approval for his leave. Next time I shall ask him to take your approval.'

'Sir, please don't do this to me. I have taken lots of pains and done lots of hard work for this competition. Please check the list once again.'

'Hello! Those who got selected have also taken pains to clear the exam. Do you feel it's only you who has taken the pains and the rest of the guys who have been selected had got it by some fluke?'

'Sir, I am not saying that, what I want to say is that I am selected and I was told this yesterday. My name has also appeared in the newspapers, I have the cutting.'

'I told you that the wrong list got published in yesterday's papers and we have published the fresh list in today's papers.'

'This is ridiculous! How could you people do this? You can't play with somebody's future! I want to meet someone in a higher position.'

'Oh, you don't believe me and you want to meet someone in a higher position?'

'Yes!'

'Then you can go and meet Mr Frini Cashen.'

'Where does he sit?'

'Do you think I am a sign board?'

'Then who will guide me?'

'I don't know, ask somebody else.'

*****

'Excuse me, can you tell me where Mr Frini Cashen sits?'

'Take the first right and then go to the last cabin.'

'Thank you, sir.'

'It's okay.'

*****

'May I come in, sir?'

'Who is there?'

'Hello, sir, my name is Sudipae. I want to talk to you about the rank list that was published in yesterday's papers.'

'What rank list are you talking about?'

'Sir, about the AlphaLand police examination results.'

'So?'

'Sir, my rank is fortieth all over AlphaLand and today I came to submit my documents.'

'So?'

'But the person who is sitting outside is saying that I am not selected and the results that were published yesterday are wrong, I just don't understand how is it possible?'

'See, boy, yesterday wrong results were published and we have published the fresh results in today's papers.'

'Sir, but how is that possible? It can't happen like this! You people can't play with somebody's future. So many people may have read those papers and they may have jumped with joy and today you are saying that wrong list got published yesterday? You people have shattered so many dreams. Now what will happen to those guys whose names were there yesterday but not in today's papers?'

'You don't try to be a leader.'

'All I want to say is my name was there in yesterday's list. I have even called Mr Sujelikae here and he, too, confirmed that to me.'

'I already told you that in yesterday's papers, the wrong list got published.'

'But how can you do that?'

'Look, you don't say to me what to do and what not to do. I know my job better!'

'This is wrong!'

'Look, I have plenty of other things to do, so please excuse me now.'

'You can't answer like this!'

'If you are not leaving then I have to call the security guys to throw you out of my office.'

'This is wrong and I shall fight for justice.'

'Please go for it, my dear fellow. It will take years before the court gives any decision. If one court doesn't give decision in your favour then you can go to the higher courts but, son, do you know the amount of energy, time, and money that you shall be putting in all these? *Haaaaa!* It's enormous. Now, if you are done with your crap then let me do my work.'

'Yeah, you are right. You have plenty of other things to do than listening to the grievances of a common man. Now may I know for what you people work for?'

'Get out, you idiot!'

'I am going, don't bark.'

'Get out!'

'Don't shout.'

'Holy shit! This phone is ringing again. Hello! Frini Cashen here who is this?'

'You idiot! What the hell do you think you are up to?'

'Good morning, sir, how are you?'

'You rascal! You don't even know what to publish and what not to publish!'

'I am sorry, sir, when this happened I was out of town or else I shall have taken corrective measures.'

'Have you not trained the buffoons working under you properly? Can't they do their job properly?'

'I am sorry, sir.'

'You dumb! Better take corrective measures or else I will throw you so far that you shall never be able to see this town again!'

'Sir, we have published fresh results in today's papers.'

'What a great work you have done. Do you want me to give you a reward for this?'

'Sorry, sir.'

'This should not happen next time or else I shall tear you apart!'

'No, sir, this is the last time. This shall never happen again.'

'Better.'

'Hello? Hello, sir? Sir?'

*****

'Hey, boy, listen.'

'Leave me alone! I don't want to talk to anyone right now.'

'Listen, boy, have a glass of water. I know you are very upset.'

'How the hell do you know what is going on in my mind? You don't have any clue! I am feeling like demolishing everything.'

'I know how you are feeling right now and what you are going through because this is what I have been seeing for so many years.'

'What are you talking about?'

'I am Rudrae and I work here as an office assistant. I have seen so many people like you who come here with a lot of enthusiasm and return with frustration, anguish, and tears. I know what they go through. The merit lists declared by these guys are on the recommendations of high profile people.'

'What?'

'Many big people are behind this.'

'If everything is pre-decided then why the written examination and other selection processes are conducted?'

'They do this to fool people.'

'What?'

'They can't do wrong things openly. They can do illegal things only in a legal way. If they don't conduct the examination and the selection processes then they will easily come into the light which they don't want to. So to avoid the controversies, they do this drama.'

'Does this happen every year?'

'Yes, every year.'

'No wonder why our nation has such a full proof security system and every now and then we become soft targets to our enemies.'

'You are right.'

'What are chances of a common person being selected on merit?'

'Son, it's almost zero. But if your luck favours you, and if you are that one in a million then you can be selected.'

'What?'

'Yes, it's one in one million.'

#####

'Sands! Sands! What happened? In which world were you?'

'Oh nothing, I was just thinking of something.'

'Gosh, Sands, I was banging your head for so long. I guess you were in some different world.'

'Oh come on, Jeans, I was just thinking of something.'

'Sands, just an advice, if you have a habit of daydreaming then just leave it immediately. Trust me, it's dangerous.'

'Jeans, I was not daydreaming okay.'

'Sands, you were.'

'Jeans.'

'Okay, fine.'

'Where are we heading to?'

'Come, I will show you.'

'Jeans, I am feeling a little tired, I want to take some rest.'

'You are tired so early?'

'Jeans, it's almost evening now. Since I have come here, I have not taken a rest. I am really feeling tired.'

'Okay, no problem, you take a rest. We shall go tomorrow to other places.'

'Jeans, can you help me in finding some place or hotel to stay?'

'Yeah, sure, let's take a cab.'

*****

'Good evening, madamae. Good evening, sirae.'

'Good evening. Please take us to Cubinaoes.'

'Okay, madamae.'

'So how is this place Cubinaoes?'

'It's quite an amazing place. You will find lots of hangouts there. There are malls, recreation centres, food joints, clubs, and the list goes on and on and on.'

'That sounds great!'

'You can have fun there.'

'I hope the hotel where you are taking me is not that expensive.'

'Don't worry, Sands, it's reasonable and best. In fact, in AlphaLand, all the hotels are reasonable and best.'

'That's interesting.'

'So here we are at Cubinaoes. Please stop the cab at the right side.'

'Okay, madamae.'

'Okay, thanks.'

'You are welcome, madamae.'

'Sands, come, let's go to that hotel. It's called Alphocubae.'

'Jeans, the hotel looks awesome! Are you sure it's reasonable?'

'Relax, Sands, let's go inside.'

*****

'Good evening, madamae. Good evening, sirae. Welcome to Hotel AlphoCubae.'

'Good evening, see I am looking for a room for him. Is there any room available in your hotel now?'

'Yes, madamae, we have single and double rooms both available.'

'Okay, then provide one single room.'

'Sure, madamae. Please fill in the details in the touch screen pad available in front of you.'

'Sands, please fill in the details.'

'You don't maintain registers?'

'I am sorry, sirae, we don't have books or registers. Please fill in the details in the touch screen pad available in front of you.'

'Sands, in AlphaLand there is a *go green concept*. As per this concept, minimal or almost negligible usage of papers has to be done and this becomes the responsibility of each and every citizen. This helps in saving trees, and the government religiously promotes this.

'Okay, no worries. I shall fill my details here.'

'Thanks, sirae, so kind of you. We hope you will have a pleasant stay here.'

'Yup.'

'Sirae, your name is Mr Saandip.'

'It's Sandeep.'

'Mr Sandeep, you have indicated that you are coming from AlphaLand but this is AlphaLand. I guess by mistake you have mentioned our country's name as yours.'

'I have not done any mistake, whatever I have written is true.'

'Okay, okay, listen, he is our guest so please take down his details and you can keep my card in case you need someone to endorse him.'

'Okay, madamae. Zinkuhae please take sirae's luggage to room number A109A.'

'Okay, Sands, you get some rest and I shall also take a leave now. My house is nearby so you can call me if you need any help. I shall see you in the morning at eight.'

'But aren't we having dinner together?'

'Well, I would have liked to have dinner but I have some work to be done at home. Let's have it tomorrow.'

'Okay then, see you tomorrow.'

'Take care, Sands.'

Chapter Three

'Swarges'

'Hi, good morning!'

'Good morning!'

'So how are you feeling?'

'Yeah, I am good. I had a good sleep so I am feeling much relaxed today.'

'That sounds great. So aren't we taking something for breakfast?'

'Of course, come let's go to the restaurant. I had dinner here last night and it was mind blowing. And the best part was, I didn't give any order, the waiter! He himself brought food for me and the food was awesome!'

'While leaving I ordered for you at the restaurant. I knew you will have difficulty in placing the order.'

'What? You have placed the order for me but you didn't inform me?'

'Well, it was a surprise.'

'That was cool.'

'Can we go to the restaurant? I am feeling hungry.'

'Sure!'

*****

'Good morning, madamae. Good morning, sirae.'

'Good morning. Can we have a table for two with a good view?'

'Madamae, please come with me this way. This place shall give you good view of the river that is flowing outside. Please make yourselves comfortable.'

'Thanks. Can we have the menu, please?'

'Yeah sure, madamae.'

'Thanks.'

'Welcome, madamae.'

'So, Sands, what would you have, *oops!* I am sorry, let me order for both of us.'

'Very funny.'

'Haaaaa!'

'Sands, why don't you order for both of us. I shall be eager to know what you shall be ordering.'

'Jeans, instead of making fun of me please order for both of us.'

'I'm serious, Sands.'

'Jeans, will you order now?'

'Okay then, let's go with fuldae urrg and vigula otaus.'

'What are these?'

'These are stuffed veggies and it tastes simply amazing!'

'Okay, but also order for me one tea.'

'And I will have one fruit juice for me.'

'Let's place our order then.'

'Sure. Excuse me.'

'Yes, madamae.'

'One fuldae urrg, two vigula otaus, one teaae cubeae with ginger, and one apple luyabaer ti juice.'

'Okay, madamae.'

'How much time it will take?'

'Just fifteen minutes, madamae.'

'Okay.'

'So, Jeans, what are the plans for today?'

'Well, it's a surprise.'

'I hope you will show me some good places.'

'Don't worry, Sands, in AlphaLand there are no bad places.'

'What?'

'Sands, this is a beautiful country and you will simply enjoy it here.'

'I hope so.'

'You will enjoy the places that I will show you. You will call them wowsome.'

'Wowsome? That's really something new.'

'Haaaaa!'

'You taught me a new word.'

'Sands, wowsome gives a wow feeling.'

'Hmmm.'

'Excuse me, madamae.'

'Yes?'

'Here is your breakfast.'

'Okies. Sands, please enjoy the breakfast.'

'Will you not?'

'Of course I will.'

'So, Sands, how is the breakfast?'

'It's good.'

'Sands, this is very famous in AlphaLand.'

'Okay.'

'Let's finish it and then we shall start our day.'

'Hmmm.'

*****

'Come, Sands, let's move that way.'

'Ah, Jeans, the breakfast was quite heavy.'

'But wasn't it delicious?'

'Yup, it was but I am not able to move myself now.'

'Sands, don't worry, you shall be fine.'

'Jeans, I am not used to this type of heavy breakfast.'

'Sands, one should always have a heavy breakfast. It gives good feeling throughout the day.'

'Oh, it was heavy.'

'Don't worry, you shall be fine.'

'So where are we going today?'

'You will find out very soon.'

'Hmmm . . .

Come this way.'

'Wow! What's that?'

'It's the public transport.'

'It looks so beautiful and what's that lady statue in front of it? What is it called?'

'She is the engine and she carries the entire cart.'

'Okay, one engine and a seamless cart of seventy-five metres—that's interesting. It looks like an angel carrying so many people. It's cool.'

'Sands, this is called the Mahas Ranni Bagis.'

'Quite a unique name, the Mahas Ranni Bagis. Are we going in that?'

'Of course we shall be going in this to the place where I am taking you now.'

'Where?'

'You shall find out.'

'When?'

'Have patience.'

'How long?'

'Come fast! The cart is about to leave.'

'Aren't we taking tickets?'

'We don't need, there is no ticket system in AlphaLand. We have stopped using it ages back and now we use Viswasae card for everything.'

'What is this Viswasae card?'

'I will explain to you, let's first get into the cart.'

'Yeah, sure.'

'We have entered at a right time, the door was about to close.'

'Yeah, lucky we are.'

'Yup!'

'Come, let's sit there.'

'Yeah.'

'You were telling me about Viswasae Card.'

'Are you seeing this card?'

'Yes.'

'This card is called Viswasae card. This is provided by the government of AlphaLand and this is unique for each and every individual.'

'Okay.'

'This card can be used in the bank, for telephone recharge, payment of electricity bills, shopping, transportation, movies, withdrawal of money, tax, and for many other purposes. In a nutshell, whatever transaction an individual wants to do, he can use this card and most importantly, this is the individual's identity card as well.'

'But how does it work?'

'See, all the details of the individual are mapped in this card and it is stored in the government's central server and this card is just like a prepaid card which needs to be recharged.'

'How you paid for me and how the money shall be deducted.'

'See, I have pressed number two just before entering, so that means I shall be paying for two people. The moment we get down from the cart the money shall automatically be deducted from my account for the two people.'

'That sounds interesting. One more thing that I noticed was I have not seen you paying the cab guy. Was that also deducted from the prepaid account?'

'Yes, every cab has the machine that reads the card. Once the passenger gets down from the cab he or she has to flash the card in the machine and the amount gets deducted from the prepaid account.'

'What if the person is not carrying the card?'

'Then that person just can't go anywhere and do anything. This card is just like a lifeline. If someone forgets the card then that person has to go and get it.'

'That's interesting.'

'If someone has lost the card then immediately it has to be informed to the police and till the time the card is found or a new card is issued, a temporary card is given to the person.'

'So the moment it is informed to the police, is the card blocked?'

'Yes. But even if it is not blocked no one can use it.'

'How?'

'The card is also mapped with the person's eye retina.'

'And what if the person wears glasses or contact lenses?'

'The machine reads the retina through the glasses.'

'What?'

******

Next station Swarges.

'Come on, Sands, the next station is ours.'

Swarges . . . Swarges . . .

'Come, Sands, let's get down here.'

'Yup!'

'So here we are.'

'What is this Swarges place? What are we seeing here?'

'Oh, have some patience, Sands, it will hardly take few a minutes to be there.'

'Hmmm.'

'I will have to blindfold you before I take you to the place.'

'What?'

'It's a surprise.'

'Jeans, I hope you are not having plans to kidnap me.'

'Can you think something good? I would like to blindfold you because I want to show you something that you have not seen before. It shall be a surprise.'

'Okay, no issues.'

'Don't worry. I am blindfolding you only for a few moments. You need to hold my hand or else you will fall.'

'Holding your hands forever.'

'What?'

'Nothing, let's go.'

'I heard you said something.'

'Well, I have not said anything.'

'Anyways.'

'But what have you heard?'

'Well, you said so lightly that I could not hear it properly.'

'I don't know what I said.'

'I hope you are not scared.'

'No, I am not but how long is it going to take?'

'Here it comes, Sands, you can open your eyes now.'

'What a fish? What is this? This is stunning! I have never seen a place like this before. It's simply breathtaking! Totally unbelievable! So many buildings in milky white colour, with mountain view at the backdrop and the river flowing across it. It's lovely! I guess I just can't stop myself from seeing it, this simply looks like some panoramic view! Oh, it just can't be natural.'

'This is Swarges, the beauty at its best. This is one of the most amazing places in AlphaLand.'

'Okay.'

'The mountains and rivers that you are seeing are natural but the buildings and their paintings are craftsmanship of humans.'

'Outstanding!'

'So how did you like the place?'

'Jeans, this is a great surprise! I mean it's beyond my imagination.'

'Yeah, it's one of the most astonishing places in AlphaLand.'

'But what is Swarges? Is it some historical place or what?'

'It is home for poor people.'

'What?'

'It comes under redevelopment program between public and private partnership.'

'What actually is that?'

'The real estate companies appointed by the government take the land from the poor people which they have been using since ages. They take the land for the construction of some commercial premises, shopping malls, hotels, offices, parks, residential buildings, and other projects.'

'But how can they take the land like that?'

'It is taken after having proper consent from the poor people and the government. In return the real estate companies and the government compensate the poor people by providing houses and other facilities at some decent locations so that the poor will not suffer. The government also takes care of the employment, basic infrastructure facilities, and any other thing that the poor can be depleted because of the change in the location.'

'So is it done only in a few locations or in many locations?'

'It is done in other locations as well. The government has some plan for the development of the poor and also on the development of localities. They work according to their plan.'

'But this kind of serene and beautiful location may not be available everywhere.'

'You are right, Sands, all the places are not blessed by nature. But wherever it is not available then it is developed through manual efforts. Like some artificial fountains are created, some lakes are made, landscapes are made and other things are done. So it is tried to make it look natural without affecting nature. During the development program the environment clauses are strictly followed.'

'*Hmmm*. Looks quite innovative and honest way to approach towards a cause.'

'Yeah, Sands, that's how our leaders work for us. The township that they develop for the poor has education facilities, basic amenities like food, electricity, water, etcetera. As I have already mentioned even job assistance is given by the government and wherever jobs are not there then it is created.'

'That's great!'

'Yup, this how poor people are taken care of in AlphaLand.'

#####

'Dingy, what is the status of the project? It's very crucial for us. You know how Mr Kans is supporting you on it and he doesn't put his money like this. He knows that you are one of the best builders and that is the reason he has put his faith on you.'

'Mr Kapats, you know it is a huge project. We are making a lot of stuff in that thirty acres plot. We are making multiplexes, commercial offices, malls and it's going to take some time. As you know, it is a prime location and some parts of the land belongs to the poor who have been staying there for ages, so we are having some difficulty in vacating them from there. First of all, they are not willing to vacate the place and if with some luck we are able to convince them then they are demanding a compensation for that.'

'Dingy, why are you guys becoming so soft on these poor people? Why don't you just throw them out of that place?'

'Mr Kapats, don't speak like an ignorant person. Nowadays it's so difficult to throw somebody out of their land. You know how fast media is today, they flash everything in a matter of a few seconds.'

'Yes, I can understand that.'

'Mr Kans has told us we shall be getting court orders for vacating those poor guys as well as he told us he shall be getting help from local authorities. These environment dumb idiots are behind us, they are saying we shall be having a tough time in getting the environmental clearance. So it is like too many things to be sorted out right now.'

'Ah, Mr Dingy, you become impatient and frustrated very quickly. The day Mr Kans has put his hand on you;

you should have stopped worrying about small things. Look at these papers that we have got for you. These are the court orders for vacating the land and with these papers we shall throw those poor chaps out of that place. Mr Kans has also got it sorted out with local authorities and the environment guys, so all the major issues have been resolved now. You can start your work now and if any issue crops up then it can be sorted out, you know it's not a big deal for Mr Kans.'

'That's great news. Now I don't think we have any major hurdle. I shall start the work very soon.'

'Mr Dingy, the stakes are high we want to give a better look to this place as foreign visitors are keeping an eye and they may visit the place very soon. We have to show them something and if things go well then there shall good inflows of foreign funds.'

'The court order says that we have to build houses for these poor people on their name in some nearby location as per the current market price of their land. But what will we provide them? We don't have any housing facility for them at this point in time.'

'Ah, Mr Dingy, don't worry about that. These guys are important vote bank for us so we have to play this kind of gimmicks with them. We can't lose our vote bank.'

'But where will we provide them the housing facilities?'

'See, your project shall be started after the elections which is due in fifteen days' time so everything has to be done after the election. Before that we have to just announce to these poor people that they shall be compensated with houses at good locations as per their existing land rates and take a consent from them in writing for acquiring their land.'

'After that?'

'We shall already be having their consent before elections and once the elections are over then who cares for them. Who the hell shall be coming and seeing what we have given and what we have not and you know there is always a scope to twist the law a little bit here and there.'

'*Haaaaaaa!* That's great!'

'This is a plot to trap them by Mr Kans. So don't worry, Mr Dingy, everyone is in our pockets. Cheers!'

'Cheers, Mr Kapats!'

#####

'Sands! Sands!'

'Oh, Jeans! Why are you shouting at me?'

'Sands, where were you? I told you to stop the daydreaming activity. I have been shouting for ages and you seem to be in your own world. I was yelling at you but you were not at all listening to me.'

'No, no, I was just looking at Swarges.'

'Then in that case, you have a very peculiar way of looking at things. You have just forgotten everything as if you are in some different world and not aware what is happening around you.'

'Oh, I am really sorry. I got engrossed at looking Swarges.'

'Are you sure?'

'Yes, of course, this place is great and it's worth coming here.'

'Okay, that's cool, but I guess we should now go to the next place that I want to show you.'

'Which place are we going? I want to be here for some more time.'

'I can understand this place is such that no one wishes to leave this place and you have also been mesmerised by it but we have to leave now or else we shall be late for the next place.'

'Oh no.'

'Come on, Sands!'

'But where are we going?'

'Sands, we are going to a very nice place and you will enjoy there as well.'

'Okies, as you say, Jeans, but can I come to this place again?'

'You can see this place as many times as you like. There are no restrictions for coming here.'

'Okay, that's good.'

'Now let's take a cab.'

'How far is the next place?'

'It will take thirty minutes. The place shall be open for another two and a half hours for the day so we may be able to spend one and a half to two hours there.'

'What's that place and why are you so eager to go there?'

'It's one of my favourite places and I have been there many times but still the desire to go there never dies. Lots of people visit there as they simply love to be there. It opens only once in ten days.'

'Okay.'

Rich and Poor Man

Hey you people get out of here
I don't want to see you anywhere near
You are a stain on this society
I don't have on you any pity

Sir, sir, sir, where shall we go
In this place our forefathers came years ago
Please don't treat us the way you are treating
We still have some self-respect left in us, if not anything

If you want us to leave
Then show us something which we could believe
Or else you leave the place and we shall stay
Because this is not your court where we will listen to
    what you say

Wait, wait, you fellow, don't get so aggressive
We are also not that submissive
Look at this notice that we have obtained from the court
Better you leave the place or else we shall sink your boat

Sir, sir, sir, the notice says that to provide us houses in
    better location
If not provided we shall not leave this place that is our
    conviction
It is easy to say we are stain
But no one has thought how much we feel the pain

People should now stop us cursing
As we are now in queue of progressing
Instead of just thinking only about your development
The time has come for you people to do something for
   our upliftment

Chapter Four

The Marro Kaminos ko Dande Stan

'Good afternoon, madamae. Good afternoon, sirae.'

'Good afternoon, we want to go The Marro Kaminos Ko Dande Stan, please.'

'Okay, madamae.'

'Come, Sands, let's get in.'

'What place did you say? The Marro Kaminos Ko Dande Stan? What's that?'

'Sands, the place is quite unique and you should experience it.'

'Let's see.'

'Please drive a little faster we are getting late. I have to show him the place, this is his first visit.'

'I am sorry, madamae, I can't drive fast. If my taxi exceeds the speed limit then I will have to pay a penalty.'

'Okay, go as per the speed limit.'

'Madamae, I don't believe that this is sirae's first visit to The Marro Kaminos Ko Dande Stan.'

'He is our guest and this is his first visit to our country.'

'Oh, that's great, sirae. Please have a pleasant stay here. Madamae, today we will have one more person who shall join the fan list of The Marro Kaminos Ko Dande Stan.'

'You are right.'

'Sirae, those who have visited the place has become its fan.'

'Jeans, tell me something about this place.'

'You shall find it very soon.'

'So you are giving a surprise once again.'

'Yup, there is always more fun in surprises. If I tell you before then you will lose the anxiety.'

'The way you people are saying about the place, I get a feel that it is one of the most popular places in AlphaLand.'

'Yes, you are absolutely right.'

'Madamae, we have reached.'

'Please stop the cab at the entrance.'

'Okay, madamae.'

'Jeans, this place looks quite crowded.'

'Yup, it is, and the next two hours shall be one of the most unforgettable moments of your life.'

'Let's see.'

'Come, Sands, let's move.'

'Have a great day, madamae. Have a great day, sirae.'

'You too.'

*****

'Welcome to the Hell. Welcome to the Hell. Welcome to The Marro Kaminos Ko Dande Stan!'

'What are these cartoons? I mean these artificial creatures? Why are they shouting at top of their voices?'

'They are electronically made creatures and their job is to welcome the visitors.'

'What are these stalls?'

'Here you get rotten eggs, tomatoes, sleepers, black paint, etcetera. You can purchase whatever you feel like buying.'

'What is the use of these stuffs and why are people buying them?'

'I will tell you. Let's purchase them.'

'You are not telling me anything.'

'Hey, you give me two packets of rotten eggs, tomatoes, sleepers, one box of paint, and two brushes. Sands, that shall be sufficient I guess or do we need more?'

'I don't understand what you are saying.'

'I guess it would be sufficient and if we are short of anything then we can purchase again. Come, let's move.'

'Jeans, where are you taking me? It's damn dark and I am unable to see anything.'

'Don't worry, walk straight for a while. We shall find the light at the end of the tunnel.'

'Give me your hand, I can't see anything.'

'Okay, hold my hand and walk straight.'

'Yeah, now it is somewhat better. But why is there no light in the tunnel?'

'Sands, it's just a twenty-five-metre tunnel. See, we have just walked for a few seconds and we have reached the end of the tunnel.'

*****

'Good afternoon, madamae. Good afternoon, sirae.'

'Good afternoon. We need two tickets, please.'

'Sure, madamae. Here are your two tickets.'

'Thanks.'

'Have fun, madamae. Have fun, sirae.'

'Sure.'

*****

'Is this run by the government?'

'Yes, this is run by the government of AlphaLand and the money collected from here is used for development and charitable work.'

'Jeans, why are these helmets kept here?'

'We have to wear them before we go inside.'

'But why do we have to wear a helmet to go inside?'

'Sands, without a helmet it shall be difficult to stand inside.'

'What?'

'Yeah, wear it and let's move.'

'Jeans . . .'

'Fast!'

'Holy shit! This place is stinking. Where the hell have you brought me?'

'I told you to wear the helmet. Wear it now!'

'Oh, fish! You said we will have a great experience. But what is this? First, we have purchased all the rotten stuffs, then there was no light in the tunnel and now we have to wear this helmet or else we may not be able to stand this smell. I don't understand what you are up to.'

'Sands, trust me it shall be a very different experience. We will have lots of fun.'

'I am already having a different and unforgettable experience which I didn't desire to have. Is this how you guys have fun?'

'Sands, believe in me we are going to have fun. Just wait for a few seconds and you shall see all with your eyes.'

'Is there anything more left to see?'

'Come, let's go.'

*****

'Oh, don't beat me. *Ahhh!* It's stinking.'

'Please give me your helmet. *Yuck!* This rotten egg smells like shit!'

Please spare me. Please pardon me. Aaahhh! Don't give me electric shocks my back is in pain. I beg you, please.

Oh! This stick is so heavy, please spare my back. Don't beat me with the stick after all I am also human like you.

'Jeans, who are these cartoons and why are they crying like this? Why are the people beating them with all the rotten stuffs? Why are the people giving electric shocks to these cartoons? I am just confused I don't know how to react, it's simply ridiculous.'

'Sands, wear the gloves and let's start using these rotten stuffs to the best of our abilities like how others are doing.'

'You mean we should beat these cartoons with rotten stuffs?'

'Of course! Yes, what are we waiting for? Look at that cartoon it looks so disgusting and no one is beating it. Let me hit it with this egg.'

'Can you tell me why we have to beat these cartoons with these rotten stuffs?'

'You will find it out, don't worry. Just do as I say, you shall simply enjoy, follow me.'

Ah! Who the hell has beaten me? Don't you know I am Narkheswea? How dare you guys touch me?

'Here's another one.'

Hey! You idiot! Why are you beating me with this egg? Oh my god! It's stinking! I will die.

'Jeans, he called you an idiot.'

'Sands, he called me an idiot and you are just listening.'

'Then what shall I do?'

'Hit him with the egg.'

'But why should I hit him, you need to tell me.'

'Because he called me an idiot.'

'Okay, here goes the egg.'

Oh! This stinks like shit. Hey, you guys! Why are you hitting me with the rotten egg?

'Jeans, now tell me who are these cartoons and why are people beating them?'

'Sands, these cartoons are the embodiment of corrupt people, criminals, and the traitors of AlphaLand. People who are beating them with the rotten stuffs are simply venting their anger.'

'Why the cartoons?'

'Because the original guys are locked in prison and no one can touch them. That is the reason why these cartoons are kept who can speak and resemble like the original ones. People are allowed to vent their anger on these cartoons.'

'Jeans, now I am going to hit him with a rotten tomato.'

'Yuppie!'

Aahh! This tastes pathetic. Hey, you jerk! What the hell are you thinking of yourself?

'Jeans, look at that cartoon, it looks very arrogant.'

'That resembles Mr Duryodhs, a very corrupt politician. Come let's nail it.'

Oh don't, please spare me. What are you people planning to do? Please leave me.

'Hi, Mr Duryodhs! Here we go, live wire!

Aaaaaaaaaaaaaaaah! Aaaaaaaaaaaaaaaaaaaaah! Aaaaaaaaaaaaaaaah! No! My back is gone. It's paining! Please stop! Please stop! Ahhh! No, no please!

'Sands, what are you waiting for? Pick up one wire and give Mr Duryodhs some more pleasure.'

'Yup, sure. Here I come, Mr Duryodhs.'

No, no, please gentleman, leave me, leave me, please! Ohhhh! Ohhhhh! My back, it's gone! Please spare me!

'So, Mr Duryodhs, how is the ride?'

Ooohhh no! Oohhhh no! Please my, son, leave me, I beg you.

'*Haaaaaaaaaaaaa!* Jeans, look at the way he is shaking its awesome. Look at his hair, my gosh, they are all standing tall!'

'Sands, come let's go there.'

'What is that cartoon?'

'He is Mr Jarasandaes the great.'

'*Hmmm.* And why is he great?'

'You will find it out on your own, come.'

Hey, babes, wassup? You look hot. Can we go for a date somewhere my, sweety?

'Jeans, what the hell is he saying? Is he out of his mind?'

'Sands, just see the fun.'

'Fun?'

'Mr Jarasandaes do you want to go for a date with me, hah?'

Oooh yeah, where shall we go, honey?

'Wherever you say.'

'Jeans, what the hell is happening here?'

Hey, ma lady how about Deep South beaches? There are lovely views there, what say you?

'Jeans, how can you interact with a cartoon like this?'

You are calling me a cartoon, you idiot, you are a buffoon.

'Hey, handsome leave him and look at me. How do I look?'

You look very gorgeous, ma lady.

'Jeans, you are asking a cartoon to judge your beauty. This is ridiculous.'

'Just be quiet, Sands, and give me two seconds.'

Ooh, ma lady, this idiot is again interrupting us.

'Hey, you don't listen to him. Just tell me how much will you give me on a scale of one to ten?'

Oohh my honey, you are ten on ten by all means. You are a dream for any man.

'Come on, don't praise me so much, I am not that beautiful.'

No, babes, I am not lying, you are an angel in this world. I am lucky that you are talking with me right now. I was wondering why haven't we met before and today when we are meeting then, is it just a coincidence or destiny?

'Come on, Jerads. *Oopps!* Can I call you that? I mean you are such a big personality hope you will not mind it.'

Ohh yes, babes, you can call me whatever you feel like. This Jerads is all yours.

'Thanks, Jerads. You are so humble and so cute.'

Thanks, babes. Anything for you.

'Jeans, now enough of flirting, done with this, Jerads.

'One sec.'

Hey, pretty, who is this guy and why is he interrupting again and again?

'Ohh, Jerads, you were telling me about Deep South beaches. What shall we do there?'

We shall go for a candlelight dinner. It shall be an awesome experience, ma lady.

'It shall be amazing.'

Yuppie!'

'Jerads, if you allow then, can I touch you?'

Come on, my lady, don't ask my permission.

'Ohhh, Jerads.'

Oohh, no! Ooh, no! This bamboo is so heavy, what the hell are you doing? It's paining. You said you are going to touch me then why the hell are you beating me? Stop it! Stop it please, my back is gone.

'You idiot! You want go with me on a date? You want to have a candlelight dinner with me?'

You only proposed.

'Come, let me take you to Deep South beaches.'

No, no, please. Spare me, please don't beat me. Oooh, my back! Somebody stop her!

'Sands, what are you waiting for? Take a bamboo and beat this swine. This jerk should not forget that there is a mom and a sister at his house as well and he should better know how to behave with ladies.'

'You jerk! I was dying for this moment. Jeans, now I will take this guy to Deep South beaches for a candlelight dinner. Come on, Mr Jerads.'

No, no, you nice man! Please don't do this. Please! Aaaahh! Oooooohhhhh! No, no, you kind man, no.

'You rascal, you flirt with young ladies and girls who are half of your age. It's shame on you!'

No, son, no, I was just kidding. No, please don't give electric shock. Aaaaahh! Ooohhh! Please, please forgive me.

'Hey, Sands, leave him now and let's go that way. I have to show you some other things as well or else we shall be busy with these cartoons only.'

'Your fate is good, you rascal, that I have to go. Now put some balm on your back.'

*****

'Sands, how did you like it?'

'Yeah, it was a really good experience, something different. In fact, I have never thought that I would be seeing something like this.'

'Great! Then I will explain to you further.'

Oooh! Plllease, plleassee spare me. Ohhh! This tomato smells so bad. Ooohh! Pleassse don't hit me with that stick, my past wound is still not healed completely. Ooooh! You man . . . no . . . no . . . aahh! Aahhh!

'Sands, let's go from here or else we shall be listening to these screams and I may not be able to explain to you properly. Let's go that side there is a cafeteria, we can remove our helmets and sit with some peace.'

'Yup! Sounds good.'

'Come on, hurry up! We have to see other things also.'

'Hmmm.'

'Here we are. *Aahh!* Now I can remove my helmet.'

'Yeah, after quite a time we are able to breathe some fresh air, Jeans.'

'Would you like to have something?'

'No, I am fine, it's all right.'

'Okay, Sands, then in continuation to what I was telling earlier, this place The Marro Kaminos Ko Dande Stan has got lots of importance for the people of AlphaLand.'

'Okay.'

'Here people don't come for fun but they actually come to show their anguish, frustration, agony, sufferings, and anger. As said earlier as well, these cartoons are not just simply cartoons but they actually resemble to each and every culprits in real life.'

'Okay.'

'These cartoons resemble to corrupt politicians, bureaucrats, employees, agents, NGOs, teachers, officials, doctors, so on and so forth. These cartoons resemble to people who have done something to defame the nation.'

'Hmmm.'

'These culprits have done corruption in allocation of telecom licenses, road contracts, misutilised public money, they have put black money in some other country to avoid the tax, they have done corruption in the education field, while generating employment, medicine, elections, you just name it and you will find these thugs involved in the scam.'

'Hmmm.'

'Sands, can you see that side?'

'What is that?'

'That is the place where the actual culprits are imprisoned.'

'It looks like a very old building with stupendous craftsmanship. The building has been given a finesse touch.'

'Yeah, the building has been designed by one of the best designers in AlphaLand. This designer has also designed many state of the art buildings in AlphaLand.'

'Okay.'

'Sands, this building is a highly guarded building. There are many world class security devices used to protect the building. The building also has the best security guards of AlphaLand.'

'Will they allow us to go inside?'

'Yes, why not? But we need to maintain some decorum and protocol.'

'What are the decorum and protocol that we have to follow?'

'We have to maintain silence, we cannot talk to anyone there. We can talk to each other that, too, in low volume. There are some restricted areas inside the building and we are not allowed to go there. We can't talk to the prisoners and neither can we make a mockery at them.'

'Okay, got your point.'

'Come then, let's go.'

'Yup.'

*****

'Good afternoon, madamae. Good afternoon, sirae. How may I help you?'

'Good afternoon, we want to enter inside to see the prisoners.'

'Madamae, the prison is open for another one hour so you can see it.'

'Okay.'

'I am handing over the escort machines to each of you guys. All the protocols are in the machine and it shall guide you to your trip inside the building. The machine shall blow horn when you try to break the protocol or when your trip time is over.'

'Okay.'

'I request you guys to go through the protocol before entering inside.'

'Sure!'

'After you go through the protocol the machine shall conduct one test and only when you pass that, you shall be allowed inside. Please make yourselves comfortable and go through the protocol.'

'Come, Sands, let's go through the protocol and take the test.'

'Are you sure I will pass the test?'

'Come on, Sands, it's not tough. I have gone through it many times so I can say it's not that tough.'

'Okay, as you say.'

'So the next few minutes let's concentrate and pass the test.'

'Yeah, let me try.'

*****

'Good afternoon, madamae. How may I help you?'

'Well, I want to enter inside the building.'

'Madamae, the prison is open for another fifty-five minutes so you can see it.'

'Thanks.'

'Madamae, before that you have to take the test.'

'Sure.'

*****

'So, Sands, how was the test?'

'I cleared it, Jeans, I don't know how.'

'I told you it's not that tough. Come, let's go, fast.'

'Yup!'

*****

'Good afternoon, madamae. Good afternoon, sirae. How may I help you?'

'Good afternoon. We have gone through the protocol and cleared our test. So can we now go inside?'

'Sure, madamae. Please have a pleasant trip and I hope you shall abide by the protocol.'

'Yeah, sure we shall abide by the same. Just one request. I have with me a guest, he has visited our country for the first time. Can I explain to him about the locations and prisoners when we tour inside the prison?'

'Good afternoon, sirae. I hope you are having a nice stay in our country.'

'Yes, officer, I am enjoying my stay here.'

'That's great! Madamae, you can explain to him but maintain the volume as prescribed in the protocol.'

'Yeah, off course, officer.'

'All the best.'

'Thanks!'

'My pleasure.'

'So, Sands, let's move.'

'Yup.'

*****

'We are inside now so maintain the protocol.'

'Wow! This place is overwhelming. Is this a prison or some king's palace?'

'Sands, in AlphaLand lots of importance are given to the design, looks, strength, and longevity of the buildings.'

'But why such an eye-catching structure is built for prisoners?'

'The area is very highly guarded with robust security systems and for that the structure has to be good. If the structure is not good then every now and then the prisoners have to be shifted which is not at all advisable.'

'Yeah, I can understand.'

'Sands, you need to also think that apart from prisoners there are police officers, guards, and other people who work here, they, too, need a good ambience to work.'

'I agree and also there are visitors who come here so for that, a good structure is required.'

'Very rightly said.'

'Jeans, why does each cell in the prison have LCD screens?'

'These LCDs gives the prisoners the actual visibility of what people think of them. What we have done outside with their cartoons can be seen by them in the LCDs. Look at that prisoner, he is seeing someone hitting him with a rotten egg.'

'Gosh! That's awesome! That means they can actually see the agony of common people.'

'They can actually see how they are humiliated by the people and that adds more insult to the injury.'

'Look! He is cursing the fellow who has hit him with the rotten egg.'

'Let him curse but he has to accept the fact that this is what people think about him and this is how people will show their anger and frustration. He needs to learn something out of it. The eggs are not thrown at him rather they are thrown at the deeds that he has done. These culprits should understand that they should not take the emotions of the common man for granted and play with it as long as they want. They should know when a common man raises then it becomes extremely difficult for these swines to bear their anger.'

'Very rightly said.'

'Come, let's go this way.'

'Yup!'

'This part of the prison is for all the corrupt officials, teachers, and NGO representatives.'

'Look at that cell, some young chap is putting rotten tomato in the mouth of the cartoon and *eeehh!* Look how the cartoon is trying to escape from the rotten stuff!'

'Sands, he is a teacher.'

'How can you say that?'

'Look at the board outside the cell.'

'Yup! That's right. The details are mentioned there.'

'Sands, the young chap may not be happy with what this teacher has done. Kids usually have high regards for the teachers, they consider them as their role models and they try to follow their teachers.'

'I agree.'

'When these teachers do the kind of activities that are totally shocking and unacceptable then the faith that these young chaps develop for their teachers gets destroyed and devastated like anything. Teachers are the one who build the society and it is highly unacceptable when they get involved in cruel activities.'

'Yeah, it's totally unacceptable when makers become destructors.'

'Let's read what's written on the board.'

Name: Mr Bhugraganian
Profile: Asst. Professor Psychology
       Gurmeadies23w's College
Crime: Attempt to rape a student
Sentence: 15 years of rigorous imprisonment
       and after release to do social work
       for 10 days a month for 10 years.

'Jeans, the great fellow is involved in a rape case.'

'Such a rascal he is.'

'Very true.'

'This fellow should never be allowed to come out of prison. In schools and colleges the teachers are considered to be just like parents but look what kind of a thing this swine has done. When you find these guys involved in such activities then one doesn't know who one should trust and who one should not.'

'Yes, that's true.'

'Come, let's go that way.'

'I hope we are adhering to the rules of the prison.'

'Yes, we are following the protocol or else the machine would have blown by now.'

'Hmmm.'

'Sands, this is the place where all the doctors, saints, priests, clergymen, and preachers who have committed crime are imprisoned.'

'It's very sad when highly revered people like doctors and saints commit heinous crimes. Saints and priests are someone who have detached themselves with all the worldly pleasure and they dedicate their life for the betterment of the mankind. It's very tough to digest when these people get involved in such activities.'

'It's not only a matter of the doctors or priests. It's anyone whom we put so much of faith and later when we find that they have committed crime then our trust and faith gets completely shattered.'

'Very true.'

'These doctors who have committed crime earn so much but their wants and desires are so big that they find other ways and means to earn more money. They get involved in illegal selling of body organs, female feticides, and many more crimes, the list goes on and on and on.'

'True.'

'These saints, who are imprisoned here, fool their followers for years. They play with innocence of common people but they forget that in the end they have to pay for their bad deeds.'

'Yeah, Jeans, at the end one has to pay for all the heinous activities that the person has done.'

'Let's read what's written on the board.'

Name: Saint Babaramae
Profile: Saint
Crime: Drugs smuggling, kidney theft and
woman trafficking
Sentence: 45 years of rigorous imprisonment
and after release to do social work
for 30 days a month for 10 years.

'Jeans, this guy has committed a very high degree of crime but don't you think he shall be very old by the time he is released, then how shall he be able to do the social service?'

'Sands, you are right but all these judgments taken by the court are based on the amount of crime committed by the guilty. Sometimes these decisions may sound unrealistic but it's purely on the level of crime committed.'

'*Hmmm.* I guess with this type of punishment people shall think ten times before committing any crime.'

'Yeah, and the whole idea is to make the punishment so harsh that people should think plenty of times before committing any crime.'

'Hey, look at that lady, how badly she is hitting Saint Babaramae's cartoon.'

*****

Lady, no, please don't beat me. Aahhhhh! It's painful! I am a saint, I am a holy man, I am a son of god. The god shall not forgive you. Don't beat aahhh! Please . . . please.

'You cheat, you have fooled us for so many years and now it's payback time, you rascal!'

*****

'Sands, look at the saint's expression while he is seeing the lady hitting his cartoon. He's looking as if he wants to kill that lady.'

'He is so brazen that he has no regrets for what he has done.'

'Yeah, such a shameless guy he is. But he is paying for his deed so it doesn't matter whether he is having any regret or not.'

'Very true.'

'Come, let's go that way.'

'Jeans, this place looks quite darker. I am scared please help me, someone please help. I am going to be kidnapped.'

'Be quite, Sands, don't crack idiotic jokes or else the escort machine will blow.'

'What?'

'Escort machine.'

'Okay, okay, I just forgot. I shall abide by the rules.'

'Better or else we shall be thrown out.'

'Yup, sure. But why is this place so dark?'

'See the lights are a little dim, maybe some repair work is going on.'

'But this may help the prisoners to escape.'

'Sands, no one dares that. They can't even open the gate of their cell, it's full proof.'

'Okay.'

'Hey, look at the signboard, it is written there to use the place carefully as some repair work is going on. They have kept the lights at appropriate locations.'

'You are right, full marks to you.'

'Yup.'

'You can't be wrong, after all you are my friend.'

'Oh really?'

'Yeah.'

'If you want then we can take a break. The cafeteria is down there.'

'No, Jeans, I guess we should move ahead as there is very little time left for the closure of the prison for the day.'

'Yeah, how can I forget that, let me check the time. Oh gosh! Let's move quickly we have little over thirty minutes left before the closure and I still have to show you some important locations here. Let's go this way.'

'Okay.'

'Sands, in this place, corrupt police and defense personnel are imprisoned.'

'Okay.'

'Apart from them, people who belong to the law and order like judges, lawyers, and security people who were involved in corrupt practices are also imprisoned here.'

'Can we have a look at some of them?'

'Yeah, of course, why not. Come, let's see.

Sure

Oh we can't see inside. The cells are closed right now.'

'But why they are closed?'

'That means some interrogation is going on. The officials may be trying to extract some information.'

'Okay.'

'Let's check his profile.'

```
Name:  Kaamkaje Kuheae
Profile: Head Police Northern left Zapivae
Crime: Involved in illegal smuggling of
       weapons
Sentence: 35 years of rigorous imprisonment.
       After release to do 25 days of social
       work once in every two months for
       45 years.
```

'See, Sands, he was the head of police at Zapivae. It's a beautiful place with lots of beaches and it is a great place for vacation. This rascal was involved in such a high degree crime in such a beautiful place. People like him are responsible to turn a beautiful place into a dugout of crime. Had I been the judge I would have tied heavy stones on his shoulders and kept him in a very dark place for the rest of his life.'

'I can understand your anguish.'

'Come this way, let's see who is this fella and what has he done.'

'This lady is a judge and look, she was involved in a paedophile case.'

'Sands, this is what irks. These people are supposed to be setting examples for the society, they give sentences to the culprits but look at this lady, how badly she has lost her principles and values.'

'You are absolutely right, Jeans. In this case the saviour herself has become the destructor.'

'Come, let's go the other side. I have to show you a very important cell.'

'Which cell?'

'Have patience.'

'Okay.'

'This is the cell. Let's read what is written on the board.'

Name: Khadoes Pape
Profile: Head of Defense AlphaLand
Crime: Involved passing confidential
       information to ZelphaLand
Sentence: Rigorous Imprisonment till death

'I guess he is a real traitor.'

'This guy, Khadoes Pape, was the defense chief. The chiefs of air, land, water, cyber, and underground defense used to directly report to him.'

'Okay.'

'Sands, the defence body in AlphaLand is an autonomous body. The government doesn't have any control on it. There is no politics, hegemony, and nepotism involved in the recruitment, promotion, demotion, and the court marshal in this institution.'

'Okay.'

'The defence head has his own powers and not even the Alpha Numero One minister can revoke or influence his decision.'

'Okay.'

'Some institutions like courts, apex bank, defense, and intelligence are completely out of the government's power and no one can touch them. If anyone is found guilty in influencing the decisions of these bodies then no one can imagine the sentence that the person has to serve.'

'Okay.'

'ZelphaLand is our neighbouring country. Its main motto is to break the peace and harmony of our nation and for that it has tried to do countless attacks but it could not succeed in any of its attempts.'

'Okay.'

'This guy, Khadoes Pape, as you have rightly said is a real traitor. He was involved in passing crucial information to ZelphaLand and you can just imagine the amount of damage that could have happened had all the information been successfully passed to them.'

'It could have done enormous damage.'

'This guy along with Zebuae Daslingisue tried to pass on the information on ammunition and on other confidential things to ZelphaLand. But they forgot that law and order is above everyone irrespective of how powerful they are and now both of them are imprisoned for lifetime till death and they can't meet and talk to anyone.'

'Who is this Zebuae Daslingisue guy?'

'He was the most coveted scientist of AlphaLand. He was considered as a father figure by many scientists, academicians, and politicians.'

'Okay.'

'Zebuae Daslingisue is imprisoned in that narrow lane. All the scientists who have committed a crime are imprisoned there.'

'Jeans, what's that place?'

'Sands, that is where culprit actors, directors, producers, and the people involved in arts and music, movies, theatres and television are imprisoned. Just opposite to that is where the culprit bankers, sportsmen, executives, media people, and other culprit people are imprisoned.'

'Okay.'

'Sands, before this place gets closed for the day let me show you the place where the corrupt politicians are imprisoned.'

'Okay.'

'Come this way.'

'Sure.'

'So here it is. This is the place where our beloved corrupt and culprit politicians are imprisoned.'

'I hope they are taking proper rest without any regrets for what they have done.'

'Yes, you are right. I am sure they don't repent, such shameless creatures they are.'

'Hmmm.'

'Sands, do you remember Jerasands?'

'How the hell can I forget him? You were flirting with him like anything.'

'I was not flirting with him I was flirting with his cartoon, okay, and it was intentional just to teach that scoundrel a lesson.'

'Tell me about him. What did he do?'

'Jerasands was the infrastructure minister.'

'Okay.'

'He was involved in allotting contracts to many companies without doing any validation.'

'Okay.'

'Later it was also proved that most of the companies belonged to his kins and he provided the contracts to them by giving them clean chit without any verification. By doing this he blindsided many prestigious companies who deserved to get the contracts.'

'Okay.'

'The materials used by these companies for the construction of the flyovers were of inferior quality and some of the flyovers even collapsed during the construction. There were lots of causalities reported.'

'Okay.'

'There was huge public outrage after this incidence. These contractors and the projects came into scanner and a special committee was setup for the enquiry. Despite being in such a powerful position, Jerasands, too, couldn't escape the enquiry. All the culprits were found guilty and they were booked for their criminal offenses.'

'But why were you flirting with him?'

'Jerasands was also caught in an attempt to rape case. He tried to rape a model who was a close friend of his daughter.'

'What? So what action was taken against him for attempting to rape a model?'

'He was suspended from his ministry post for a year. Enquiry happened but nothing came out of it, so he was reinstated again in the ministry.'

'So this fellow is a big time rapist.'

'You are right. I was trying to flirt with his cartoon to express my anger and I knew he shall fall for it.'

'*Hmmm . . .*'

'Let me also tell you about an incident that once happened while he was addressing a public rally.'

'What was the incident?'

'The media was at its best, the entire national channels were covering the event and millions of people were listening to the speech that he was giving while addressing the rally.'

'Okay.'

'During the speech he took out his handkerchief and to everyone's astonishment, ladies panties came out of his pocket. All the news channels flashed the news instantly and it became a nationwide gossip.'

'What?'

'Yes, it was a big embarrassing moment for him.'

'Jeans, see how intently he is watching on the LCD the people beating his cartoon.'

'Let the swine watch. He can't go back to work neither can he have girls so this is the only stuff left for him now.'

'True.'

'Sands, you remember Duryodhs?'

'Yeah, I remember that arrogant guy.'

'He is imprisoned in that cell.'

'So what did he do?'

'He was involved in allotting mineral mines to many companies in an illegal way. There are various procedures and steps to allot these mines to the companies but he bypassed all the laws and procedures.'

'Okay.'

'He allotted these mineral mines to the companies that offered him lots of benefits and kickbacks. He was caught for his criminal offense and now he is behind bars for rest of his life.'

'Okay.'

'Sands, in AlphaLand the corrupt people are not spared and they get for what that they have done. No one is above the law and one has to pay for one's bad deeds.'

#####

'Silence please. Silence please.'

'What steps have been taken by the honourable minister to bring the black money back to AlphaLand?'

'Yes, tell us the steps that are taken by the government on this. We need answers today, you can't avoid these questions. Tell us honourable minister.'

'Please maintain silence. Silence please. Please sit down. Silence please. Mr Nathanae, you are requested to take your place. Mr Nathanae, please sit. Mr Godi Pandeyae, please take your place. Please maintain silence.'

'Tell us the steps that are taken by you. You can't ignore this. We need your answers now.'

'Please maintain silence. Silence please.'

'We need answers. The honourable minister has to answer this. This question can't be avoided.'

'You all are requested to take your respective seats. Please don't make a crowd near the well. You are requested to go back to your place.'

'We need answers today. The honourable minister has to answer today.'

'Silence please. Kindly go back to your places.'

'We need answers.'

'Okay, the parliament is adjourned for the day.'

'The parliament can't be adjourned like this. The honourable minister has to answer today.'

*****

'Mr Kittoes, every time we raise the question about the black money the parliament gets adjourned. I don't know how long it will happen like this. Why is the government not taking stringent measures to bring back the money? It can be utilized for our country's development. Why is the government zipped about it?'

'Mr Sulaes, there are many ministers, bureaucrats, corporate honchos, officers, and many other powerful guys involved in this black money scam.'

'Okay.'

'The government doesn't want to do anything because they know that if they take any step then lots of hidden things shall come out and the government will collapse.'

'*Hmmm . . .*'

*****

'Long live Winnae Vijarea! Long live Winnae Vijarea!'

'Friends, this government can't deny its responsibilities. They have to answer to the people. They have to tell us the modus operandi about how they shall be bringing the black money back to the nation. The government can't shy away from this. We are not going to leave them till the job is done.'

'Long live Winnae Vijarea! Long live Winnae Vijarea!

'Friends, they say that I am involved in corruption. I throw an open challenge to them to prove about my involvement in corruption. What the hell can they prove? I have not allowed even a single stain on my character and reputation till now.'

'Long live Winnae Vijarea! Long live Winnae Vijarea!'

'If they can prove that I am guilty then I shall leave my protest and serve sentence that the court decides for me. But if they can't then they have to do what we say. They have to bring back the black money to AlphaLand.'

'Long live Winnae Vijarea! Long live Winnae Vijarea!'

'Friends, these thugs feel that I am old and alone. But they don't know that the entire nation is with me. We need the answers. We will not let them go, we shall fight against these goons till our last breath.'

'Long live Winnae Vijarea! Long live Winnae Vijarea!

*****

'Mr Goel, what the hell is this, every time these opposition guys raise the black money issue. Why are these guys so serious about it now? Why haven't they done anything when they were in power? These guys just want to mislead everyone.'

'You are right, Mr Kalhotra.'

'When these guys were in power then they did only those things that were favourable to them and now they want everything to be done.'

'Mr Kalhotra, it's not only the opposition who are after us. There are others as well.'

'What do you mean?'

'Lots of protest is going against us across the country. The nation is demanding answers about the black money.'

'*Hmmm.*'

'Specially this man, Winnae Vijarea, he is trying to bring awareness to the public about the black money, corruption, and other critical issues. I heard he is getting lots of support across AlphaLand and if these protests become successful then we all are in a fix.'

'*Hmmm.*'

'Opposition is always behind us and they are seeing this as an opportunity to crush us. Lots of guys from opposition are also involved in the black money scam and now they are raising their voice to just politicise the matter and get some benefits in the election.'

'You're right.'

'I guess we need to talk to the high command, only he can do something about it.'

'Yes, Mr Goel, let's discuss this with the high command. I will call his personal assistant and make an appointment.'

'Sure.'

*****

'Hello, Mr Chatke.'

'Hello, Mr Kalhotra, how are you doing? What a pleasant surprise!'

'I am good. Mr Chatke, can we meet the high command today?'

'What is the reason, Mr Kalhotra? I hope everything is fine.'

'No, Mr Chatke, not everything is good. Something has to be done or else very soon we shall be in doldrums.'

'What are you saying?'

'Need an urgent appointment with him. Please tell me when we can meet him today?'

'He is having a meeting today with the prime minister and the home minister on some very confidential issue and then he is leaving in the early morning for Zingolu for a vacation. So in the next ten days there is no possibility for the meeting.'

'When will the meeting be finished?'

'I can't tell you the exact time but it may go on till two in the morning.'

'Mr Chatke, please understand that this is very urgent.'

'Mr Kalhotra, I can understand but I am afraid I may not be able to help you.'

'Please understand, Chatke, everyone is after us. If nothing is done then this government may collapse.'

'What are you saying?'

'I am serious.'

'Let me check with sir and then I will call you.'

'Okay, I am waiting for your call.'

'What did he say, Mr Kalhotra?'

'He will check with high command and call back.'

'Okay.'

'I wish we can meet him today.'

'Is it doubtful?'

'Well, he is having some important meeting with the prime minister and the home minister and after that he is going for a vacation.'

'That means we may not be able to meet him.'

'Let's hope for the best.'

'Yes, let's hope for the best.

See Chatke is calling. I think he had a word with the high command.'

'Pick up the phone.'

'Yeah, Mr Chatke.'

'Mr Kalhotra, I spoke with, sir.'

'Okay.'

'He has given an appointment at two in the morning.'

'You mean right after the meeting with the prime minister and home minister?'

'That's true.'

'Okay, we shall be there. Thanks for the help.'

'My pleasure, see you then in the morning.'

'Sure.'

'What happened?'

'Meeting is fixed for tomorrow morning at two.'

'What?'

'Yeah, we have to be there in the morning.'

'But it's too early in this winter.'

'Goel, we have no option as he is going for a vacation after that.'

'Okay.'

'I hope the issue gets resolved today.'

'Yes, Mr Kalhotra, or else the government shall collapse.'

'You are right.'

'If this black money issue ignites further then everyone shall be gone. Whatever I have shall be seized.'

'Relax, Goel, the high command will come up with some solution.'

'I wish something happens or else I have to pack up my stuffs and leave this place forever.'

'Goel, don't get so worried, everything shall be fine. We are not here to leave this place, we are here to make money for us, for our family, and for our coming generations. These black money and other issues will come and go but it can't deter our motive to make money.'

'You are right.'

'Goel, we have time left before the meeting starts so let's go somewhere.'

'Where?'

'Let's go and freshen up somewhere.'

'*Hmmm.*'

'I guess you got my point, you bad boy.'

'You family man, let's go. Where are you planning to go?'

'Remediesea. All nice and young chicks are there.'

'*Hmmm.* That sounds good.'

'We will take my car and leave yours here.'

'But don't you feel it's risky to take an official car there?'

'Don't worry, it's a personal car.'

'You bring your personal car as well to the parliament.'

'Well, most of the time but it is parked at a reserved parking area that I obtained at nigeoaer at the other side of the road.'

'That's interesting.'

'Well, one can't use an official car for this purpose.'

'I agree with you.'

'Let me call the driver.'

'Sure.'

*****

'Hello.'

'Yes, sir.'

'Where are you? Bring the vehicle, fast.'

'Yes, sir, I shall be there in five minutes.'

'Why five minutes? Where the hell are you?'

'Coming sir.'

'Come fast, you idiot.'

'Yes, sir, I am there in a moment.'

'What happened?'

'The car is coming.'

'Okay.'

*****

'I have to go now as Kalhotra has to go somewhere urgently. He is shouting at me.'

'Same old story. You know, Shreea, where he wants to go.'

'You know it, Vikramae?'

'You know why Kalhotra always shouts at you?'

'Why?'

'Because whenever he goes there to have fun, his fate ditches him.'

'*Haaaaa!* Okay now I am going or else he is going to kill me.'

'All the best.'

*****

'How much time this fellow is going to take to bring the car?'

'Mr Kalhotra, there he is, coming.'

'Good afternoon, sir.'

'Where the hell were you? I told you not to roam anywhere then why did you go?'

'I was there only, sir.'

'Shut up!'

'I am sorry, sir.'

'What sorry.'

'Kalhotra, let's go or else we shall be late.'

'Take us to Remediesea and make it fast.'

'Yes, sir.'

'Kalhotra after Remediesea, let's go to the Jacksea to have food there.'

'Good idea.'

'We have a good fourteen hours left with us before the meeting starts, so let's make the most of it.'

'You are right, Goel, let's spend some eight to nine hours in Remediesea and then we will have dinner before we go for the meeting.'

'Sure.'

*****

'Good evening, sir.'

'Good evening, Suvid, how are?'

'I am fine, sir. What can I do for you?'

'You know it, Suvid.'

'Of course, sir. Give me five minutes, I will arrange everything for you. Please make yourselves comfortable.'

'Okay but make it fast.'

'Sure, sir.'

'Goel, let's have drinks by that time.'

'Good idea.'

'Excuse me.'

'Good evening, sir. How can I help?'

'Bring two large rum with lemmone juice and one plate of chicken lollipops for us.'

'Sure, sir.'

'Goel, let us enjoy ourselves completely here.'

'Yes, Kalhotra, let's rock.'

'Excuse me, sir, sorry to interrupt you in your discussion.'

'Not at all, Suvid. Is everything ready?'

'Yes, sir, everything is ready as per your choice.'

'Then why are we wasting our time here. Suvid, we have ordered some drinks and snacks can you arrange to send them in our respective rooms?'

'Sure, sir.'

'Do not disturb us for the next eight hours and whatever we need we will order in our rooms.'

'Sure, sir.'

'So can you take us to our respective rooms?'

'Yes, sir.'

'Goel, let's have fun then.'

'This way, sir.'

'Sure.'

'Kalhotra, we are going to have a great time here.'

'Yes, Goel.'

'Sir, here are the rooms.'

'Both the rooms are side by side, right?'

'Yes, sir.'

'That's good, Suvid.'

'My pleasure, sir.'

'Goel, go and enjoy yourself.'

'You too, enjoy yourself, Kalhotra.'

'Cheers!'

'Cheers!'

*****

'Ah! Who is calling me now?'

'Hello? Hello?'

'Ah! Hello?'

'Hello, Goel, it's one in the morning, let's move fast or else we shall be late.'

'Ah! What happened, Kalhotra? Why are you sounding so worried?'

'Goel, we shall be late, hurry up now and you know high command is very particular with time. See you in five minutes at the entrance.'

'Ah! Give me ten to fifteen minutes.'

'We don't have time, get up fast!'

'Ah! Listen, Kalhotra.'

'Goel, you have only five minutes, come fast.'

'Okay, babes, got to go, bye!'

'Bye, sir, but when are we meeting again?'

'Suvid shall let you know.'

'Okay, sir.'

*****

'Where are you? Bring the car at the entrance.'

'Yes, sir.'

'Sir, I hope everything was as per your expectations.'

'Thanks, Suvid.'

'My pleasure, sir.' When shall be your next visit, sir?'

'I will let you know.'

'Sure, sir.'

*****

'Yeah, Kalhotra, I am here.'

'Let's move fast, the car is ready.'

'Sure.'

'Take us to 8 Mountae Road.'

'Yes, sir.'

'Goel, I guess we have to skip Jacks or else we shall be late.'

'Yeah, I am not feeling that hungry, Kalhotra, it's okay with me.'

'Oh gosh! You are stinking, Goel. How much did you drink?'

'Ah, not much.'

'I think you should skip this meeting. It shall be not advisable for you to attend the meeting in this state.'

'Ah, don't worry, Kalhotra, I will manage.'

'Are you sure?'

'Yeah.'

'Don't speak much there and be careful.'

'Hmmm.'

'How much more time will it take to be there?'

'Five more minutes, sir.'

'Make it fast!'

'Kalhotra, how was your evening?'

'It's not the time to talk about all this.'

'Mine was great.'

'I can see that.'

'It was real fun.'

'How much more time? You rascal, drive fast!'

'We have reached our destination, sir.'

*****

'Open the gate we have an appointment with sir. Please hurry up!'

'Security check, please, you need to get down from the car, sir.'

'Oh come on! We come here so often.'

'Sorry, sir, but security check is a must.'

'Come on! Allow us to go inside.'

'Sorry, sir, you shall have to get down from the car.'

'Come, let's get down quickly, Goel.'

'Yeah.'

'Sir, please come one by one.'

'Okay.'

'You are done, sir, you can come this side.'

'Okay.'

'Check the car as well.'

'Okay.'

'Are they clean?'

'Yes, sir.'

'Please hurry up, we shall be late.'

'Open the bonnet and the doors.'

'Yes, sir.'

'Is it clean?'

'Yes, sir. Clean.'

'Check through the sensors.'

'Don't treat us like this, you know who we are?'

'Sorry for the inconvenience but we can't help it.'

'Do it fast.'

'Anything detected?'

'No, sir. It's clean.'

'Allow them in.'

'Finally.'

'Thanks for your cooperation, sir.'

'Drive to the entrance.'

'Yes, sir.'

*****

'Good morning, sir.'

'Good morning!'

'Please come this way, sir. Mr Chatke has asked you to make yourself comfortable here.'

'Sure.'

'Mr Chatke shall be here in a while.'

'Can we get some water?'

'Sure, sir.'

'Kalhotra, how long we shall have to wait?'

'I think the meeting is still going on so we have no option but to wait. I suggest you don't open your mouth much, it's literally stinking.'

'Ah, come on, you know too much of boozing at this age has its own fun. So how was your experience?'

'Can we talk about this later?'

'We are sixty but we are still so energetic!'

'Goel, be quiet now.'

'I had two pills and everything was fine.'

'Goel, go and wash your face and have some mouth freshener.'

'If everything had been in my hands then I would have married her.'

'What?'

'But suddenly pictures of my wife and children came into my mind and I had to drop the idea.'

'Goel, now stop your crap.'

'Kalhotra, you know I was a Casanova when I was young . . .'

'Be quiet now.'

'Who is coming?'

'Mr Kalhotra, Mr Goel, come, let's go for the meeting, sir is waiting for you people.'

'Sure, Chatke.'

'Come.'

'Goel, have this mint and don't open your mouth.'

'What happened, Mr Kalhotra? Is there something wrong?'

'Goel is drunk and I am suggesting him not to come but he is insisting to be the part of the meeting.'

'Mr Goel, Mr Kalhotra is right. I also suggest you don't go for the meeting, sir will not like it.'

'Oh come on, you guys. I am all right and there is no issue at all.'

'Mr Goel, please listen to us.'

'Come on, don't worry, I am fine.'

'Are you sure?'

'Yeah.'

'Let's go or else we shall be late.'

'Yup!'

*****

'May I come in, please?'

'Come in.'

'Good morning, sir.'

'Sit down.'

'Thank you, sir.'

'What is the issue? Why the hell did you want to meet me so urgently that you could not even wait for a few days?'

'Sir, there is some serious issues raised in the parliament about black money.'

'So what? We have also raised the issues when we were in the opposition.'

'Vijarae is also doing mass protests about black money, corruption, and other issues. He is getting tremendous support across AlphaLand.'

'Why are you so worried about Vijarae? Let him do the protests. These protests shall die down soon, don't bother yourself much on this. These things happen and is this what you called the meeting for? 'Our coalition partners are making some plot to collapse the government. I got this information from some reliable sources.'

'Tell me in detail.'

'Sir, the opposition is raising lots of questions about the black money and almost throughout the week the parliament got adjourned for the entire day.'

'I know about it, Kalhotra.'

'Sir, this is a plot by the opposition to defame us in front of the entire nation.'

'Tell me something new. Don't waste my time like this.

'Information that I got from my sources are that the party chiefs of our coalition partners TV2, 1FT, and R3T are in regular touch with opposition party leaders and they are planning to collapse the government. They are looking for midterm polls.'

'What?'

'Sir, the opposition is playing with the black money card. They are constantly provoking our coalition partners with these issues and trying to break our strength.'

'What kinds of discussions happen in the meetings?'

'Sir, I can't give the exact details but they are discussing issues like the black money, corruption, license allotment scam of the mines, rise in commodity and fuel prices and other prices.'

'What else?'

'They have already convinced our partners TV2, 1FT, and R3T and together they are planning to bring these issues in front of the people in a much bigger way. They are preparing a strategy of collapsing our government. I heard the master plan is ready.'

'What?'

'Yes, sir.'

'What else?'

'To add insult to injury, Winna Vijarea is also not leaving any stone unturned. Every now and then he is doing some public meetings and rallies. It is heard that the opposition party workers are also trying to enter his rallies voluntarily.'

'What else?'

'Sir, something has to be done now or else the situation shall be completely out of control.' 'Everyone shall be ruined that is the reason we have asked Chatke to arrange for this emergency meeting.'

'Damn! It's stinking. Are you drunk? How the hell can you come in the meeting like this?'

'Ah, sir.'

'You don't even think where you are going and with whom you're having a meeting?'

'I am sorry, sir.'

'Go and wash your face. I don't want to see you in this meeting anymore.'

'Please forgive me, sir. I am extremely sorry. I will not repeat this mistake.'

'Chatke.'

'Yes, sir.'

'Take Goel to the wash room and I don't want to see him in this meeting anymore.'

'Yes, sir.'

'Please forgive me, sir. I beg you.'

'Come, Mr Goel, let's leave.'

'Goel, get out! It's an order. Chatke, take him out.'

'Yes, sir.'

'Kalhotra, how the hell Goel has come for the meeting when he is drunk?'

'I told him not to come for the meeting. Even Chatke has suggested to him the same.'

'I just don't believe this. How did you let it happen?'

'I am sorry, sir.'

'He will have to face the repercussions and I am leaving you with a warning.'

'I am sorry, sir.'

'Let's get back to work.'

'Yes, sir.'

'Whose sources are these who are giving the information?'

'Both mine and Goel's.'

'How trustworthy are they?'

'They can be trusted completely.'

'What do you think?'

'I think we should have a meeting with these party chiefs as they are our important coalition partners and if they withdraw their support then we shall be out of power.'

'How many seats do we have now?'

'Fifty-seven.'

'If these parties withdraw their support then how many seats will we have?'

'Around forty-five.'

'That means six short of the magical figure.'

'Yes, sir.'

'In that case we have to talk to them.'

'Do you think we can stop them, sir?'

'No one is clean. If they know about our loopholes then so do we know about their loopholes.'

'Yes, sir.'

'Give me some time. I shall let you know.'

'Okay, sir.'

'Send Chatke inside.'

'Sure, sir. Have a nice day, sir.'

'Are you sure? Will I have a nice day now?'

'I mean . . .'

'Send Chatke.'

'Yes, sir.'

*****

'Chatke!'

'Yes, Mr Kalhotra?'

'Sir has called you.'

'Okay.'

'Where is Goel?'

'He is at the reception. He is scared and crying like anything.'

'Let me see him, I will drop him to his house.'

'Okay.'

*****

'Sir, please have some water.'

'No, thanks.'

'Goel, come let's go now.'

'Kalhotra'

'Wipe off your tears first.'

'Is he unhappy? Please tell me what happened inside?'

'Frankly speaking, I can't say anything now but, yes, he has definitely not taken it nicely.'

'What he is going to do?'

'I don't know.'

'I am scared.'

'Come, let me drop you to your home.'

'Kalhotra, please say something.'

'Goel, let's go now.'

'Kalhotra, what will he do?'

'Stop sobbing like a kid and let's move now.'

'I am finished.'

*****

'Take us to Sanjoei Road.'

'Kalhotra, what was he saying about me?'

'Goel, if you can't digest drinks then why do you have it? Do you know how unkempt you were looking?'

'Why didn't you tell me then?'

'I have told you for the umpteenth time. Even Chatke told you but when did you listen to us?'

'Now what will happen?'

'I don't know. He didn't say anything.'

'He will ruin my political career, let me go and apologise to him now. I will fall on his feet and beg for mercy. Please turn the car.'

'Wait, Goel, don't do anything now, it will be like adding more fuel to the fire. He is not in a good mood so just wait for the right time and then apologise.'

'Why have I done this idiotism? I should have listened to you people.'

'Chatke is calling.'

'Please pickup. I guess he may have something for me.'

'Yeah, Chatke.'

'Mr Kalhotra, sir has asked you to come to his place today by 1:00 p.m.'

'But you said he is going for a vacation.'

'Well, as of now he has only told me for the meeting with you at 1:00 p.m. and one more thing, Mr Goel is not required for the meeting.'

'What?'

'Yeah, that is what he said.'

'But you know Goel is repenting for his mistake, please convey this to sir.'

'Mr Kalhotra, these are his instructions and you know no one can go against it. I feel we should follow it.'

'But, Chatke . . .'

'Sir is calling me, I have to go. See you then in the afternoon.'

'Sure.'

'Kalhotra, what happened? What was Chatke saying?'

'He said sir wants to meet at 1:00 p.m.'

'Okay then, I will come to your place by 11:30 a.m. and together we will go.'

'He said only I am required for the meeting.'

'What? Kalhotra, please do something! Take me also to the meeting. I will fall on his feet and beg for mercy.'

'I can't do anything now.'

'He is angry at me, please do something or else my career shall be ruined. Please understand.'

'Goel, I can't do anything now.'

'Kalhotra, please take me along with you.'

'Goel, try to understand.'

'Please, Kalhotra.'

'Well, I am saying no but still if you insist then come at your own peril and I shall not be responsible for anything.'

'Thanks, Kalhotra. I will never forget your help.'

'Come to my place by 11:30 a.m.'

'Sure.'

'Sir, we have reached.'

'Stop near the main gate.'

'Okay, sir.'

'Okay, Goel, take some rest.'

'Bye and see you at 11:30 a.m. at your place.'

'Yeah.'

*****

'Good afternoon, Mr Kalhotra.'

'Good afternoon, Mr Chatke.'

'Mr Goel, what are you doing here?'

'Well, Mr Chatke, I came to meet, sir.'

'Mr Kalhotra, I said to you that only you are required for the meeting then what is Mr Goel doing here?'

'Well, Mr Chatke, I know that but Mr Goel has insisted to come here.'

'You guys know that no one can go against the orders of the high command. Right now he is so angry at Mr Goel that he doesn't even want to listen to anything about him.'

'Mr Chatke, please try to understand that Goel is very much scared. I hope you can understand what is going through in his mind.'

'I can understand that but you both know that nothing is there in my hands.'

'At this moment we need your help, Mr Chatke. Please request to sir that Goel has come and he wants to apologise for his behaviour.'

'Kalhotra, he is going to kick me if I will tell him that Goel has come to meet him. I can't take his wrath, I am sorry. Today he is not in a great mood.'

'What happened?'

'There are lots of other issues and after your meeting he had to cancel his personal trip. He is not going for his vacation.'

'He has cancelled his trip?'

'Yes, and I can't take the risk of telling him that Mr Goel wants to meet him. He will throw me out of this place.'

'Come on, don't say that, please help Mr Goel.'

'Mr Kalhotra, I have my limitations. I am not a big fellow like you guys. I am an ordinary person who runs his family from this job. Please forgive me, I can't risk my job.'

'Then what is the solution?'

'Why don't you try, Mr Kalhotra?'

'Ah, now you are pushing me forward.'

'No, I am serious. You are close to the high command, why don't you try?'

'Okay, then let me see.'

'Mr Kalhotra, I will also come with you.'

'Goel, wait here, don't come right now with me. I will call you later.'

'Mr Kalhotra, please hurry up for the meeting, sir may be waiting for you.'

'Yeah, sure. Goel, I will call you.'

'I will wait.'

*****

'May I come in, sir?'

'Yeah.'

'Good afternoon, sir.'

'Take your seat.'

'Thank you, sir.'

'Kalhotra, I guess whatever you have said was very important and if proper action is not taken then things can turn worse and who knows, it can go out of our hands.'

'You are right, sir.'

'I called you for something important.'

'Yes, sir.'

'I want you to arrange a meeting with the TV2, 1FT, and R3T party chiefs.'

'Sure, sir.'

'Arrange the meeting at the earliest and if possible arrange it by tomorrow. From our side the people who shall be required for the meeting are myself, Gatotke, Dashasan, and yourself.'

'Okay, the prime minister and the home minister shall be also there in the meeting.'

'That's what I said.'

'Yes, sir.'

'Arrange the meeting at some neutral venue. It should be out of public and media eyes, I want it to be a clandestine affair.'

'Yes, sir.'

'You may leave now.'

'Sir, can I say something.'

'What?'

'I know you will not like it.'

'What?'

'Sir, actually Goel is waiting outside. He has come to apologise for his behaviour.'

'I don't want to see him.'

'Sir, I request you to meet him once.'

'Kalhotra, don't advise me. You may leave now and send Chatke in.'

'Yes, sir.'

*****

'Mr Goel, please calm down.'

'Mr Chatke, why has Kalhotra not called me yet?'

'Chatke, sir is calling you.'

'Mr Kalhotra, please help Mr Goel.'

'Kalhotra, what happened? Have you talked about me? Shall I go in?'

'Chatke, I said sir is calling you.'

'Yeah, sure.'

'Kalhotra, please tell me what high command has said about me.'

'Goel, he is not in a good mood. When I talked about you then he blasted me like anything.'

'Now what shall I do?'

'You have to wait. You can meet him only when he wants to meet you.'

*****

'Mr Goel.'

'Yeah, Mr Chatke.'

'Sir is calling you inside.'

'Chatke, how is it possible? He has just blasted me when I mentioned Goel's name.'

'Well I don't know Mr Kalhotra, but the moment I went in he asked me to send Goel.'

'It's really hard to believe?'

'Goel, what are you waiting for? Hurry up!'

'Yeah, sure.'

'Well, it's really tough to understand high command, Mr Chatke.'

'Let's see what happens, Mr Kalhotra.'

'Hope everything goes fine with Goel.'

'I hope so.'

*****

'Sir, may I come in, please.'

'Come in.'

'Sir, I am really sorry for my behaviour. It was an idiotism that I have done, please forgive me.'

'Oh, really, do you feel sorry for your behaviour?'

'I beg you for your forgiveness. I swear on my family that never in my life shall I repeat this mistake.'

'Goel, you know I can destroy you.'

'I beg for your mercy, sir. Please forgive me. I have a family.'

'Why didn't you think about your family when you were drunk?'

'Sir, I lost my mind and I have done a grave mistake. Please forgive me and give me one more chance. I shall do whatever you say.'

'No chance of forgiving you, Goel.'

'Please, sir, I beg for your mercy. Give me one chance.'

'Are you sure?'

'Yes, sir.'

'Goel, I heard your son is doing some business.'

'Yes, sir, he has just finished his management studies and now he is into textile business.'

'Okay and I guess your daughter is a doctor, right?'

'Yes, sir, she has just completed her MD.'

'Must be a bright girl?'

'Yes, sir, she has always been an outstanding student.'

'So what about her marriage?'

'Sir, we are looking for a decent guy for her.'

'How old is she?'

'She is twenty-five years old.'

'Nice age to get married.'

'Yes, sir.'

'I heard she is very pretty.'

'Yes, sir.'

'Goel, actually my son wants to meet your daughter.'

'What?'

'You heard me.'

'Is there anything important that Mr Indraejis wants to discuss with my daughter?'

'You ask too many questions, Goel. Just send your daughter to him.'

'Sorry sir, if my questions are bothering you. I will come with my daughter and meet Mr Indraejis.'

'Send only your daughter.'

'But, sir, I have never sent my daughter alone anywhere.'

'Don't worry, she will be fine. Send her tonight.'

'In the night why, sir?'

'Goel, one more question and you are gone.'

'But sir . . .'

'Send your daughter tonight and you may leave now.'

'I am sorry, sir, but actually my daughter is not keeping well.'

'No more excuses, Goel, and you may leave before my mind changes.'

'Sir, please forgive me and my daughter. Please, sir, I beg your mercy.'

'Children have to pay for their parents' wrongdoings. It's your daughter's time to pay for your deeds.'

'I beg you, sir, please forgive us.'

'Don't hold my legs and leave now.'

'Please, sir, please.'

'Chatke, please come in and take Goel out.'

'Yes, sir.'

'Sir, please forgive me. Please forgive . . .'

'Come, Mr Goel.'

'Chatke, please tell sir to forgive me.'

'Come, Mr Goel, let's go. Come.'
'Sir . . . Sir . . .'

*****

'Mr Goel, please make yourself comfortable. Suhane, get one glass of water for Goel.'
'Chatke, please help me.'
'Relax, Mr Goel. Where is Kalhotra?'
'He has left for some urgent work.'
'I have to call him.'
'First, relax a bit then you can call Kalhotra.'

*****

'Hello? Hello Kalhotra!'
'Yes, Goel.'
'I am screwed.'
'What happened and why are you crying?'
'He wants my daughter for his son's entertainment.'
'What?'
'Yes, he said to send her tonight.'
'What are you saying?'
'I don't know what to do. Please help me, please speak to sir.'
'Where are you now?'
'At sir's place.'
'Get out of there and don't talk about anything there.'
'What should I do, Kalhotra?'
'Do as I say. I am disconnecting the phone now.'
'Hello, Kalhotra? Kalhotra?'

'Mr Goel, please have water.'
'No, I don't need it. Please help me.'

*****

'Hello?'
'Hello, Chatke?'
'Yes, Kalhotra.'
'Chatke, ask Goel to leave for his home immediately and please do as I say.'
'Has he brought his car? I guess he came along with you.'
'Yes his car is there outside.'
'Okay, I will do the needful.'
'Thanks!'
'Suhane, please call for Mr Goel's car.'
'Sure, sir.'
'Mr Goel, come let's go.'
'Chatke, please help me.'
'Come, I will take you to your car.'
'Chatke, please speak to sir.'
'Come, Mr Goel.'
'Chatke, I am ruined.'
'Please get into your car.'
'Chatke.'
'Bye, Mr Goel.'
'Chatke, please listen to me. Chatke.'

*****

'Hello, Mr Kalhotra?'

'Yeah, Chatke.'

'He has left.'

'Thanks, Mr Chatke. I will speak to him.'

'Yes, please do, he is in a devastated state.'

'Okay, I will call him.'

*****

'Hello, Kalhotra.'

'Goel, are you on your way home?'

'Kalhotra, I am ruined.'

'Calm down.'

'That rascal Indraejis is a rapist. How can I send my daughter to him? Please save my daughter.'

'Goel, calm down.'

'Kalhotra, please save my daughter.'

'Goel, honestly speaking, you don't have a choice.'

'What are you saying?'

'You know that no one can revoke his decision.'

'But what about my daughter?'

'You have to send her.'

'How can you say this? She calls you uncle.'

'I know you are shattered but you have no option. Do as he says or else your entire family will vanish. Don't you remember what happened to Shadrenil and his family? He and his entire family disappeared in a single night, so don't try to do anything against his wish.'

'I may not be able to show my face to my daughter for rest of my life.'

'It's better than losing your entire family. 'Bye.'

'Hello, Kalhotra? Please don't hang up the phone. Please help me! Please!'

*****

'Good evening, sir.'
'Yeah, tell me.'
'I have arranged for the meeting.'
'When is it?'
'Tomorrow evening at nine.'
'Where is the venue?'
'Toes fry. Bungalow number 1309.'
'I hope it is as per what I have instructed to you?'
'Venue is as per your requirement, completely guarded and out of public eyes.'
'See you then tomorrow.'
'Yes, sir.'

*****

'Take left you idiot and stop there.'
'Yes, sir.'
'Blow the horn, you swine!'
'Yes, sir.'
'Who is there?'
'Open the gate!'
'But who is this?'
'Did Kudheran inform you?'
'Oh! Yes, sir. Good evening, sir. I am Albert Singe.'
'Open the gate.'
'Yes, sir.'

'Where is the caretaker?'

'Mr Alboleo has gone inside to check the arrangements.'

'Some guests shall be arriving in ten to fifteen minutes' time, so see to it that they have no problems in coming here.'

'Sure, sir.'

'Drive to the porch.'

*****

'Good evening, sir. I am Alboleo.'

'Have you checked the arrangements? Is everything fine?'

'Yes, sir, all set and done.'

'Few guests are expected in another ten to fifteen minutes so can you be at the gate to receive them?'

'Sure, sir.'

*****

'Open the gate.'

'Yes, sir.'

'Good evening, sir. I am Alboleo.'

'Can you tell me which way to go?'

'You need to go near the porch, sir.'

'Is there anyone to attend?'

'Yes, sir.'

'Take the car to the porch.'

*****

'Good evening, sir.'

'Where is the meeting?'

'Please come this way, sir.'

'Good evening, Mr Kutilychi.'

'Good evening, Mr Kalhotra.'

'I hope you have located this place without any difficulty.'

'Yeah, it was not difficult to locate this place.'

'Please come this way.'

'I hope I am not late.'

'Not at all, others have also just come.'

'Oh, that means I am late.'

'No, no, Mr Kutilychi, you are on time.'

'Who else have come?'

'Except Mr Dunioa everyone else is there.'

'That means Mr Shakunibe, Mr Dustovya, Mr Gatotke, and Mr Dashasan are already present.'

'Yes, Mr Kutilychi.'

'Good evening, Mr Kutilychi.'

'Hey, good evening to you all!'

'Okay, you guys, make yourselves comfortable. I am there near the porch to receive Mr Dunioa.'

'Sure, Mr Kalhotra.'

*****

'Stop the car here.'

'Yes, sir.'

'Good evening, sir.'

'Kalhotra, where is the meeting?'

'That room, sir.'

'Have all come?'

'Yes, sir, they are waiting for you.'

'*Hmmm.* So everything's set and done.'

'Yes, sir.'

'Then let's go inside.'

'Sure, sir.'

*****

'Good evening, Mr Dunioa.'

'Good evening to all of you and my apologies for being late.'

'Oh come on, you are always on time.'

'That's so kind of you, Mr Kutilychi.'

'It's my pleasure.'

'Let's have our seats gentlemen.'

'Sure, Mr Dunioa.'

'Gentlemen, first of all I would like to express my gratitude to all of you for coming for this meeting on such a short notice.'

'We knew it has to be something very important, so we could not afford to avoid this meeting.'

'Thanks Mr Shakunibe for being so considerate.'

'It's my pleasure.'

'Gentlemen, it has been quite a time since we had some good and fruitful discussion. I think for our coalition's future, for our common agenda, and for other important aspects we should have this kind of a meeting once in a while.'

'You are right, Mr Dunioa.'

'Thanks, Mr Dustovya.'

'It's my pleasure Mr Dunioa.'

'Gentlemen, we are the prominent leaders of the most important parties of AlphaLand. Whatever we think and we decide impacts the present and future the country. The main agenda for today's forum is to design a road map on how we can work together in a much progressive way in the coming years and time. I guess you all are with me on this.'

'Yes.'

'Gentlemen, there are lots of things happening around in recent times. There are issues like slump in the economy, corruption, scams, black money issues, terrorism, and the list goes on and on and on.'

'All of them are serious and major issues, Mr Dunioa. We have to also see what we have done on these fronts and what better we could have done?'

'You are very right, Mr Shakunibe. I appreciate your thoughts.'

'Mr Dunioa, the inflation is at its peak, never in the history of our nation had the inflation been so high. The spending of common man has increased in leaps and bounds in the past few years. These are all pain areas and may affect our vote bank.'

'Mr Kutilychi, inflation is at peak everywhere in the world. No country in the world is spared by it. In recent months we have taken measures to bring it down and we are optimistic that we shall be successful in curbing it down.'

'Look at the prices of fuel, cooking gas, and all the basic commodities it's at skyrocketing heights. There is no mechanism for controlling it.'

'The fuel prices and other prices are affected by global policies, it's not completely in our hands. Till now we have provided these commodities at subsidised rates but now most of our oil companies and gas companies are bleeding so we can no longer provide these commodities at lesser rates.'

'So many taxes and excise duties are levied on these commodities and these make these commodities more dearer.'

'Mr Dustovya, we are taking steps to bring them down. Even you, are in the committee that is working towards this.'

'There is no development work happening. If some road is built then it doesn't even last for one year. So many bridges and flyovers fell down during the construction phase itself. The common man is now asking questions regarding the government's spend on these projects. The common man wants to know what happens to the money that gets deducted from his or her salary in the form of tax. What answers do we have for them?'

'See if so many development activities happen then of course in few cases there shall be some issues. We are trying to put the best people in the job.'

'The cases of rapes, female feticides, and other crimes are on high. Every now and then there are mass protests going on and questions have been asked about the government's inability to act on these issues. What answers do we have for them?'

'Mr Kutilychi, strict measures have already been taken. Tough laws are made so that the guilty is not spared. Cameras and lights are installed everywhere and security has been tightened.'

'Everything is on the papers.'

'You know it takes some time to implement but very soon it shall be done. Orders have already been given for the same.'

'Mr Dunioa, every now and then your party ministers give fresh jolts. They are involved in scams, corruption, and now the fresh thing has started the black money issue. These are not small issues and your ministers have lost their credibility.'

'Mr Shakunibe, committees have been set up for the probe and they are doing their job. Nothing can be said right now as our ministers are not yet proven guilty.'

'The committee is yours, the system is yours, so everyone knows what would be the results.'

'Mr Dustovya, who said the committee is ours? These committees are genuine and are chaired by distinguished personalities of their respective fields. I can only say that you should not listen to the rumours.'

'What steps have been taken to bring the black money to AlphaLand? If black money is brought then so many development activities can happen.'

'Mr Kutilychi, we have already initiated the process to bring the black money to AlphaLand. A special committee has already been formed for this. You know it's not that easy and it will take some time for bringing the black money to our country.'

'For everything, Mr Dunioa, you have only one answer and that is the committee has been formed and it is doing its job. Frankly speaking now these things can't work. Now people are losing their faith on us. There are so many protests going on and people are demanding answers.

'Gentlemen, I give respect to your thoughts. I liked the way you people have talked about all these issues and about the worries of common man. We know we are capable of doing the development work and also we are capable enough to provide solution to the worries of the common man.'

'But we are not finding anything concrete right now.'

'Gentlemen, you know we are having some plans and we are working on it. Very soon we shall have the results.'

'I am sorry to say but people are losing faith in this government and the image of the government has been tarnished very severely. At every nook and corner of the country discussions about the scams, corruption, and black money issues are going on. People are even saying that this government shall break all the records related to scams and corruption and will create a history.'

'Gentlemen, these are all temporary things and very soon you shall see that all these issues shall be vanished.'

'Now even public wrath against the government is quite visible. There are lots of mass protests happening against the corruption and scam in recent times. Various social activists are quite active and they are also getting the response from common people. You can see the kind of response Winna Vijarea is getting from the public. There is a common feeling that this government can be dissolved anytime.'

'Gentleman, we know there are some confidential meetings happening to dissolve this government but you should know one thing—that our government is not that weak that anyone can come and dissolve it.'

'Mr Dunioa, what do you mean by that? What meetings are you talking about? Please be specific about what you want to say.'

'Okay, then gentlemen, let me be specific. We came to know that you people are meeting with the opposition party leaders and they are trying to convince you to break this government.'

'What rubbish! Who told you all that?'

'It's not rubbish, Mr Shakunibe. We have our sources who give us the information.'

'It's true that once or twice we have met with the opposition party leaders but what is wrong in that.'

'You are our coalition partners and we respect you for that, but you can't meet the opposition parties like that.'

'Come on, Mr Dunioa, we are your coalition partners but that doesn't mean that we can't meet anyone and this meeting was not at all to plot any conspiracy to break this government.'

'You can meet but why should the meeting be clandestine?'

'See, we didn't have any of kind of closed door secret meetings with the opposition but, yes, if we want to have then nothing can stop us. We are your coalition partners and if we find anything that doesn't fit our core values then we can take back our support.'

'Mr Kutilychi, if you have any problems then we can sort it out with discussions.'

'Mr Dunioa, we have discussed so many times about issues related to black money, fuel prices, scams, and other things. Every time we just got assurance but nothing concrete happened. We have to give answers to the people in our respective constituencies and we can't procrastinate.'

'See, I assure you that something concrete shall happen very soon.'

'Mr Dunioa, again you have given the same answer that you give us every time, so no point in discussing on this. Let me tell you one more thing, that coming days are not good for this government.'

'Okay, then gentlemen let me make it straight. See everyone has loopholes so if you know ours then we also know yours. My request to you people is that let's not play with each other's loopholes.'

'What do you mean by that?'

'Mr Kutilychi, before joining politics you were a doctor by profession, right?'

'What do you want to say by that?'

'We have the records of the number of female feticides cases you were involved into. How much loyal you were with your profession and for a few extra bucks how you used to sell your integrity and values as a doctor are needless to mention. We also have records of how many disproportionate assets you have and if we bring this to the notice of people, then it shall take you years to come out of it.'

'Mr Dunioa, you are bringing personal things into public.'

'Okay, then let me talk about the professional things. When the so called previous government SCVOT23i was formed in alliance with your TV2 party then many of your elite ministers were involved in numerous of scams. The cases against them are still running in the court and the verdict is getting delayed because of us. If those issues are rekindled then how many votes you will get in future only heaven knows.'

'Why are you talking about all those things?'

'We don't want to talk but you are leaving us with no other options.'

'What do you want?'

'You know what we want. Stay with us and reap the fruits.'

'You can't pressurize like that.'

'Oh, let me come to you, Mr Dustovya, the so called party chief of 1FT. Sir, we have the count of the child abuse and rape cases against you and your party members. My god, how can I forget the involvement of your daughter in the drug trafficking case. Your daughter was studying abroad, right?'

'What do you want to say?'

'You call yourself as a messiah of the poor then Mr Messiah, if I bring all the scams related to electricity, water, and land that you and your party leaders were involved into when you were in power then how many poor people will vote for you can only be counted on fingertips. Nobody likes the dirty things to come out and I think you are a smart guy.'

'What do you want?'

'Do I have to say?'

'I am with you.'

'Now last but not the least Mr Shakunibe, our so called R3T party chief. We have records of the fake medicines that your company used to supply and because of which so many people lost their lives. Allow me to tell you about your nexus with a terrorist organisation and women trafficking groups. Involvement of your party in the mineral scams and most important of all, about your role in the fuabe serial blasts is not hidden to us.'

'Mr Dunioa, why are you talking about all these things right now?'

'Guys, you people are talking about the black money stuffs but if the account numbers of the people in the foreign banks are displayed then only heaven knows what shall happen. No one will be spared, so stop politicising this issue.'

'Mr Dunioa, what do you need from us?'

'Mr Kutilychi, this is not the time to fight. This is the time to unite and take some concrete steps for ensuring the better future of our coalition government. The more we stay together the more powerful we become. So stop falling in the trap of the opposition guys and show some smartness.'

'We agree with you.'

'So can I take this as a final word from you guys?'

'Yes.'

'Thank you, guys, and let's celebrate for the better future.'

'Sure, we agree in unison.'

'Kalhotra!'

'Yes, sir?'

'The arrangements for the meeting are not proper.'

'I beg your pardon, sir, if I have missed out anything. But everything has been arranged as per your wish.'

'Then where are the things that are required for the celebrations?'

'Oh, I am so sorry, sir, please give me a second.'

'Fast!'

'Mr Dunioa, you knew the outcome of this meeting right.'

'Any doubts, Mr Shakunibe?'

'Excuse me, Mr Dunioa, I have something to say.'

'Yes, Mr Dustovya.'

'I guess Mr Suchritrae can create problems.'

'What makes you to say that, Mr Dustovya?'

'Suchritrae is clean and he has the support from some other parties as well. So he may try to break this government.'

'I appreciate your concern, Mr Dustovya, but we have made our calculations. We shall still have the sufficient numbers even if Mr Suchritrae goes with the opposition.'

'I hope your calculations are not wrong.'

'You know my calculations are never wrong.'

'I agree.'

'It's my pleasure, Mr Dustovya. So people, it's party time! Let's rock!'

'Hurray!'

#####

'Sands! Sands! The security guy is yelling at us. We have to leave. It's closing time.'

'What?'

'In which world have you gone? I was shouting at the top of my lungs but you were totally indifferent to me.'

'Madamae, it's closing time now.'

'Sorry, we are leaving. Come, Sands, let's go.'

'Yeah, sure.'

'Sands, I have observed one thing that whenever I show you something you tend to go in some other world. Why it is like that?'

'Jeans, there is nothing like that.'

'It's quite obvious.'

'I don't understand what you are trying to say, but anyways what's next now?'

'You are trying to change the topic.'

'No, I am not.'

'Okay, leave it.'

'That's what I am trying to say. Can we discuss what the next agenda is?'

'See, I will show other important places tomorrow as we may not be able to see them properly today because it's already late now.'

'Okay, no issues but where are we going tomorrow?'

'That's a secret.'

'Again the same answer.'

'But one thing is for sure, that you shall be enjoying, so don't worry.'

'Okay, let's see.'

'Sands, you didn't tell me, how did you like The Marro Kaminos ko dande Stan?'

'It was good, I had a different experience. I mean I haven't seen anything like that before.'

'Sands, whoever comes here finds it different and enjoys the trip.'

'The most that I enjoyed was when people were beating the cartoons.'

'Ha! Most of the people visit for that only. They want to vent their anger by beating the cartoons.'

'Yeah, it was quite obvious.'

'Yup!'

'So where are we going now?'

'To your hotel, I shall drop you there.'

'That means after dropping me you will go to your house.'

'Yeah that's right.'

'Now come on, Jeans, this is not done. Let's go out somewhere. Let's go to some movie and then for dinner.'

'Sands, it shall get very late. Let's plan on that some other day.'

'Jeans, come on, let's go out somewhere today!'

'Aahhh!'

'Come on, don't think too much.'

'Okay then, let's go to moviefoodie.'

'What is that?'

'You said for a movie, so let's watch there.'

'Sure, let's move then.'

*****

'Good evening, madamae. Good evening, sirae.'

'Good evening, can you take us to moviefoodie rl please?'

'Sure, madamae.'

'Jeans, I hope there is some good movie there.'

'It's a new movie and I heard it's doing well.'

'Okay, so what is the movie all about?'

'Well, it's an emotional movie. It's about a dog and an old man.'

'Okay.'

'It's about a relationship between a street dog and an old man whom the old man hates first but later finds out to be his best pal.'

'Okay.'

'Madamae, we have reached moviefoodie.'

'Okay, please stop there.'

'Sure, madamae.'

'Thanks. Come, Sands, let's go.'

'Where is the movie hall?'

'In front of you.'

'Oh! This giant glass structure?'

'Yes.'

'What is this cartoon running on the glass structure?'

'It's the mascot.'

'Interesting.'

'Come otherwise we shall be late.'

'Okay.'

'Come this way.'

'So, again, no need for tickets as the same shall be deducted from your card.'

'Yeah, you are right, but only when the seats are available inside the hall.'

'*Hmmm.* So are the seats available?'

'Yes. I have already checked so we can go inside.'

'Sounds good.'

'Yup.'

'Jeans, this looks like a big dining hall.'

'Yes, this is a movable dining hall with screens.'

'*Hmmm.* This looks great.'

'That is the reason it is called moviefoodie.'

'I guess here one can enjoy food by watching a movie. I mean this gives a kind of a restaurant feel.'

'Sands, in this place you can do whatever you feel like doing.'

'Like what?'

'You can watch a movie and at the same time you can eat and sleep, there are beds available.' 'You can bath and watch a movie, you can play and watch a movie, etcetera, etcetera.'

'What?'

'There are separate sections, you can see there and the prices vary accordingly.'

'*Hmmm.* Sounds quite interesting.'

'Yeah.'

'So when will the movie start?'

'In a while.'

'And when do we order the food?'

'No need to order. Our order is booked with the ticket.'

'Oh, great!

'You can trust me, the food shall be good.'

'Okay.'

'Hey, Sands, the movie begins.'

'*Hmmm*. Let's enjoy the movie then.'

'Sure.'

*****

'Bogoyoe, where are you?'

'Hey, you old man, what are you doing here?'

'Hey, you kind man, have you seen my little baby bogoyoe? I am looking for him and I don't know where he has gone.'

*****

'Hey, Jeans, why are you crying?'

'Nothing.'

'Come on, Jeans, it's just a movie.'

*****

'You can't leave me, bogoyoe. What will I do in this big world without you? Take me also with you. Oh my lord, please, don't do this injustice to me. Give me my bogoyoe back.'

*****

'Stop crying, Jeans.'

'I am not crying.'

'Come on, Jeans, the movie is now over. Just stop crying it's after all, a movie.'

'Can you give me the water?'

'Sure.'

'Thanks.'

'Just take it easy.'

'The climax of the movie was very touching. The old man was just craving for the dog and the dog was gone.'

'Yeah, it was touching.'

'Sands, is this what happens? One gets separated from the loved ones in the end?'

'Not always, Jeans.'

'But most of the time, it happens.'

'I am not sure but yeah, the movie was good. You made my evening.'

'Thanks, Sands.'

'So what's next?'

'Let me drop you to the hotel and then I shall leave for my home.'

'Okay.'

*****

'Good evening, madamae. Good evening, sirae.'

'Good evening. Hotel Alphocubae, Cubinaoes, please.'

'Okay, madamae.'

Chapter Five

Sache Ramn Hall Speech

'Good Morning, Jeans.'

'Good morning.'

'So how are you? I hope the movie's effect is not anymore on you?'

'Hey, I am good. What about you?'

'Yeah, I am doing great.'

'I hope you had a good sleep, Sands.'

'Yeah, of course.'

'I am sorry, Sands, I could not join you for breakfast. My mom insisted to take breakfast at home as we haven't had breakfast together for the past few days.'

'Was your mom not in town?'

'Yes, she was out of station for some work.'

'Oh, okay.'

'So are you ready for today's adventure?'

'Yes, but where are we going today?'

'Today I will take you to a place where you shall have some interesting experience.'

'But where are we going?'

'You will find out soon.'

'Again you are creating the same suspense.'

'Come, let's cross that lane.'

'What's there after that lane?'

'Have patience you will see it soon.'

'You are so good in creating suspense. Do you work with some detective agency or what?'

'Sands, look there.'

'Wow! What is that?'

'That is called SuperTrans network. It's the public transport that we quite often use in AlphaLand.'

'Oye, cool. It looks so good.'

'Yes.'

'So aren't we catching one?'

'Yeah, of course, come we need to go to platform number two.'

'Where is platform number two?'

'See it's written over there.'

'How are the people able to walk between the platforms? Where are the tracks?'

'See, when the SuperTrans is not at the platform then the special quality cement plates spread over the tracks and people walk on it and cross the platform. When the SuperTrans is about to arrive then alert signals are blown and instantly the poles come down and block people from walking on the cement plates. Once the SuperTrans arrives at the platform the special quality cement plates uncovers the tracks, the poles go up and people enter inside the SuperTrans.'

'That sounds very amazing. I guess lots of money must have been invested on this?'

'See, the government doesn't think twice in investing on something that helps people.'

'Sounds good.'

'Look at platform number three, the signals are blown and see how the poles are coming down.'

'Yeah, and the people have also stopped crossing the platform.'

'See how the cement plates are uncovering the tracks as the SupeTrans is arriving at the platform.'

'The sight looks great.'

'Yup. Come, Sands our SuperTrans is expected in a few moments.'

'Okay.'

'Here it comes.'

'Let's get inside fast or else we shall not find place to sit.'

'What?'

'I mean it shall be crowded, right?'

'Eh, don't worry there shall be ample seats, Sands.'

'Okay.'

'Come, let's go that side.'

'It looks quite empty. I guess it's not the rush hour?'

'It's peak hour, Sands. Whatever time you travel you shall always find a place to sit.'

'Okay, that's cool.'

'Yup!'

'Jeans, the SuperTrans is moving quite fast.'

'It goes with a speed of 550 mile per hour.'

'It's quite high a speed for a local transport.'

'Sands, it just flies.'

'Amazing!'

'Sands, I am having one café de nomi, would you like to have something?'

'Are there vending machines inside the train?'

'Yes, there are refreshment points.'

'Okay, I shall have whatever you suggest.'

'Sure. Let's have one each then.'

'Yup.'

'It tastes awesome.'

'Yeah, the taste is quite good.'

'Sands, we have to get down at the next stop.'

'It came so soon we just got inside the train.'

'I told you we are travelling at 550 miles per hour.'

'Hmmm.'

'Come, let's get down.'

*****

'Jeans, there are huge shopping malls here.'

'People enjoy shopping at AlphaLand and it is so convenient shopping here. One has to just shop and board the SuperTrans.'

'So are we going to shop?'

'That we can do anytime, but now we have to go to somewhere else.'

'Where?'

'Allow me to take you there.'

'Hmmm.'

'Come this way.'

'I hope it shall be a different experience.'

'Of course, yes.'

'Let's see.'

'Are you seeing that place?'

'Yes.'

'We have to go there?'

'It's so big and why are so many people are gathering there? That place looks like some huge castle.'

'This place is for public gatherings and meetings. Mr Hall is coming today and that is the reason it's so crowded.'

'Who is Mr Hall?'

'He is the Alpha Numero One minister.'

'What is Alpha Numero One?'

'It means no minister in government of Alphaland is above him.'

'Hmmm.'

'He is simply amazing. You should listen to his speech, he is our champ. People simply die for him.'

'What? People die for a minister? I have never heard of anything like that before.'

'He is such a gem.'

'Come on, all these ministers are one and the same.'

'What you do mean by that?'

'Well, basically, these ministers are drowned in corruption and in all types of scams. They make fake promises, they speak flowery words and when the time comes to deliver then they show their back and run away.'

'See, I don't know about what you have experienced before but in AlphaLand it's not like that. If a minister is caught in any kind of illegal practices then he or she is not spared. Here, no one is above the law. Secondly, we very well know whom we should elect as our leader and whom we should not. I guess you yourself should see whom we have elected and then all of your questions shall be answered.'

'Jeans, I am not interested. I know it shall be boring.'

'Come on, just see once.'

'Ah, no, please spare me.'

'Come on, hurry up! Or else we shall be late.'

'No please . . .'

'Please, Sands, just for one time.'

'Ah, okay, but if I don't like then I shall leave in the middle of the speech.'

'Okay.'

'Are we going this way?'

'Yup! You are right, Sands.'

'Jeans, it looks very different inside. Is this a public gathering place or some sort of a palace? I haven't seen this kind of public gathering place till now!'

'Isn't this place great?'

'What else do you need, this place has everything. Fully air conditioned, plush green ground, lovely leather seats, so many water coolers, and food joints. Here, it's not like people are waiting for the ministers under the hot sun for hours with no food and water. Here, it's just like party and enjoy.'

'Sands, all the PGPs in AlphaLand are like this.'

'What is a PGP?'

'Public gathering place.'

'So what's the sitting capacity of this place?'

'10 lac people can sit at a time.'

'It's quite spacious.'

'There are ten floors and these floors surround the podium. Each floor has sitting capacity of one lac.'

'That's huge!'

'Yeah.'

'How many PGPs are there in AlphaLand?'

'Well I can't give you the exact number right now but there are many.'

'It's worth coming here if not for your leader then at least for this place.'

'You should first listen to our leader before passing your judgments.'

'Whatever.'

'Anyways, let's take a seat in the second floor, we shall have a good view from there.'

'It doesn't matter what place we are sitting at as I am not that interested in the speech. I know it shall be boring and all the fake promises shall be made by the minister.'

'Again, you are trying to be judgmental. I think you have already developed some kind of notion about the politicians.'

'I have already told you not to trust them.'

'I think today your thought for them shall change.'

'I don't think so.'

'Let's see.'

*****

'Good morning, madamae. Good morning, sirae.'

'Good morning.'

'Which floor do you wish to go?'

'Second floor, please.'

'Sure, madamae.'

'So, Sands, today you shall have some different experience.'

'I don't think so.'

'Second floor, madamae.'

'Come, Sands, there are a few vacant seats there.'

'Okay.'

'This place shall give a good view.'

'Let's see.'

'Come on, Sands, don't keep any preoccupied notions.'

'Well, whatever I have experienced about the politicians that only I told.'

'But all the politicians are not the same. In AlphaLand people worship the politicians.'

'What?'

'Yes, they are just like gods.'

'I just can't believe this!'

'It's true.'

'Anyways, but when is your leader coming? I guess almost all the people have gathered inside.'

'He shall be here very soon.'

'Yeah, I know all these leaders always keep people waiting. Unless they make people wait for hours they don't get a feel that they are politicians.'

'No, it's not like that our leaders are always on time.'

'It doesn't seem like that.'

'*Shhhh!* I guess he is coming they are announcing something.'

*****

'Guys, I know you all are eagerly waiting for this moment but now your waiting time is over and here comes the moment. Ladies and gentlemen, hold on your nerves and allow me to welcome our beloved leader, the rocking hero, Mr Sache Ramn Hall. Applause, please.'

*****

'Oh god, this guy is making the announcement as if some super hero is coming.'

'Sands, he is no lesser than that.'

'Eh? Look at the way the people are screaming and why the hell are you too screaming at the top of your lungs, Jeans?'

'Sands, look he is coming!'

'I can't see him.'

'There, you idiot, at the top, near the tenth floor. Look at the open elevator he is coming in that.'

'Gosh! He is coming from the top?'

'Yeah, there is a helipad at the top of the building. His chopper has landed there and he is straight away coming from there in the elevator.'

'It's so filmy he is coming from the top in an elevator and people are going mad. Such a crap it is. This guy is taking complete rock star kind of a feeling.'

'What?'

'Nothing. I guess he is coming down.'

'Yeah, look how people are dying to touch his hand.'

'People are going crazy.'

'I think we should have come a little early. We would have gotten the front row and I would have also gotten a chance to touch his hand.'

'Do you really want to touch his hands?'

'Of course, yes. Till now I never got a chance to touch his hands and today also I missed it. I hope someday I shall be able to do it.'

'Hey, see, he's wearing slim fit trousers in red colour with yellow checks, blue shirt, and green googols. Is he a leader or some disco dancer?'

'Shut up! He is the champ.'

'Oh, this place is bursting with noise, people are simply going mad. When will they calm down?'

'Sands, this is the charisma of this man. This shows the respect that this man commands.'

'Hey, why suddenly it's so silent? What happened?'

'He is about to begin his speech.'

*****

'Good afternoon, my dear ladies and gentleman. How are things at you end? I trust all is well.'

'Yeah! Yeah, all is well! Hall! Hall! Hall! You rock! Hall! Hall! Hall! You are the king!'

*****

'Jeans, this is becoming like a musical theatre with chants of Hall.'

*****

'Hey, guys, come on, don't embarrass me with these chants. I am your servant.'

'Hall! We love you! Hall! You are our hero! Hall! You are the best!'

'Thanks a lot people for this lovely gesture. Gents and ladies it has been a long time since we have met. First of all, I express my gratitude to you all for coming here. I am honoured.'

'We are also honoured. Long live Hall! Long live our hero!'

'Thanks, people, once again. I guess you guys are doing well both professionally and personally.'

'Yeah, we are. Long live Hall! Long live Hall!'

'That's great! Guys, I hope you are enjoying the early part of the winter?'

'Yeah, the weather is great, hope you are also enjoying the same.'

'Yes, I am very much enjoying it.'

'Long live Hall! Long live Hall!'

'My dear people, the snacks are getting served so please enjoy the stuff at your seats and with you permission let me also grab mine.'

*****

'Jeans, what kind of speech is this? I have never seen a politician having snacks and giving the speech.'

*****

'Guys, just before I was coming here someone told me that the snacks are going to be good but I feel they are awesome.'

'Oye! Yuppie! Oye! Yuppie! Oye! Yuppie!'

'Okay, now the work time. I know you people are waiting for the results of what we have done on what we have promised you last year. Guys, last year was really good for us and we have done a lot of stuffs. We are happy to announce that the results are good. Most of the details you also know because all the results whether good or bad are always highlighted by the media and also they are available in our official website.'

'Agreed. Agreed. Agreed.'

'Guys, allow me to show the presentation slides of the work that we have done in the past one year.'

*****

'Jeans, what is he talking about? Is he going to show the presentation?'

'Yup, Sands.'

'Is this some corporate meeting or what? I have never heard of a leader showing presentations.'

*****

'People, I request you to look at the screens in front of your seats. The presentation is displayed in there.'

*****

'Are we watching some movie in some flight or what?'

'Sands, can you be quiet and look at your screen, please?'

****

'So my dear ladies and gents, here is the performance details in the category of power and water. Like all the previous years the power cutoffs and water shortages across AlphaLand were zero. In the remote areas we have sliced the power rates by 60 per cent to support the irrigation.'

'Yuppieeee! Good going! Yuppieee!'

'People, there have been global crisis in fuel this year. I know we have promised to reduce the fuel prices but due to global effect we were unable to do the same. As the fuel prices are at skyrocketing level so we had no option but to increase the price by 5 per cent.'

'Booooooooo! Not done! Not done!'

'Hold on guys, please hold on. I am not finished. We have increased the fuel prices but we have brought down the taxes in automobiles by 4 per cent. We have tried hard and this is what the best we could do at this juncture but I will assure you that next time we shall give better results.'

'Better show next time! Better show next time!'

'Guys, we had to also increase the cooking gas prices by 30 per cent but we have come up with a unique offer which till now no other nation has thought of. The offer is like for every two cylinders that you purchase the third cylinder shall be given at a discounted price of 50 per cent and it is not like you need to purchase these cylinders at one go. You can purchase them as and when it is required.'

'Cheers! Cheers! Cheers!'

*****

'Jeans, this guy is damn smart. He knows how to present good work and subdue the bad work.'

*****

'Guys, we are doing well on road infrastracture. We have completed 95 per cent of work of upgrading the roads from 16-lane to 18-lane roads. Balance 5 per cent we are lagging behind because of some statutory checks from the environmental department and some delays from the vendors. We have already initiated necessary action based on the reports of the enquiry committee. For some of the vendors and contractors who were not doing a good job, we have already terminated their contracts and imposed penalties on them. My dear people, we have appointed new vendors and contractors based on the opinion poll results that we have received from all you guys across AlphaLand.'

'Not bad, Mr Hall. Not bad.'

'Guys, we have increased the efficiency and frequency of SuperTrans across AlphaLand. The SuperTrans is now available every four minutes and the fare has also been dropped by 10 per cent.'

'Cheers! Cheers! Cheers!'

*****

'Jeans, is it some budget session or what?'

*****

'Guys, we could not do much on food commodities as you know there was significant drought that hit AlphaLand and because of which there was a drop in the production. But people, I salute to the resilience power of our farmer brothers and other people in locations where drought has hit. The way they are trying to come out of it is really commendable. I request to all you people to give thirty seconds standing ovation to these champs.'

'Cheers! Long live our farmer brothers! Long live AlphaLand! Long live the people! Long live AlphaLand!'

'Thanks to you all. My dear people, the government has already initiated the support to our farmer brothers and other people in the drought hit regions and very soon the things shall be fine. We have good amount of food commodities in the government Godowns that we normally use for the exports. We have cut down the exports this time by 35 per cent so that our domestic needs are fulfilled without having impact on the prices. Happy fooding, friends.'

'Yupieesss! Hall! Hall! Hall! You simply rock! Hall! Hall! Hall! You simply rock!'

'My dear people, next month we shall be having inauguration of the 21st research and development centre for defense equipments of AlphaLand and also the inauguration of the much awaited Dosties networks, the road that connects us with SinglesLand.'

'Goodies! Rock in roll, Mr Hall! Hall! Hall! Hall! You simply rock!'

'Very soon, opinion poll link shall be floated. Please send your choice about the people who shall be doing the inaugurations.'

*****

'Jeans, what is this SinglesLand and what is this opinion poll link?'

'SinglesLand is a country around 2000 kilometres north eastern side of AlphaLand. In between AlphaLand and SinglesLand a country called Ziabuaeae comes. This road network is the connectivity between AlphaLand, Ziabuaeae, and SinglesLand. This is an initiative by the government of these three nations.'

'What shall be the use of this road connectivity?'

'This shall be used to support trade and tourism. In addition to this, people of these three nations can meet their relatives and dear ones. The transportation cost will also be lesser.'

'But travelling 2000 kilometres by road shall be a difficult task.'

'Sands, when the vehicle will hit at 400 odd miles per hour then it shall not be difficult.'

'But what is this opinion poll link for inauguration?'

'The inauguration shall be done by selected representatives of these three countries. To choose the representative from AlphaLand, the opinion poll link shall be floated so that people can express their choice on this link.'

'Do they float this kind of opinion poll links every time?'

'Yup! People's choice is always taken for any event, project, and initiative.'

'That sounds good.'

*****

'My dear people, this year the number of scams and scandals have been very few. In fact, only one scam took place and that was related to electricity production. The culprit has already been punished based on the court verdict.'

'Cheers! Good Job! Good job!'

'People, despite being a developed economy we are growing at tremendous rate. Our growth rate is far higher than any other developed country.'

'Bravo! Hip! Hip! Hurray!'

'Guys . . .'

#####

'See, there comes the chopper.'

'Gosh! It's so noisy my ears are gone. Look, it's all dust, nothing is visible.'

'Mr Damnky's chopper is almost landing. Have you checked the car that will take him to the podium? Is it ready?'

'It is ready.'

'Better check once again.'

'Sure.'

'Quick!'

'Hey, you idiot, is the car ready? Mr Damnky's chopper is about to land.'

'Yes, sir, it is ready.'

'Anything goes wrong you know the consequences.'

'Yes, sir.'

'So how are things? Is the car ready?'

'Yes, sir, the car is ready. I have checked everything.'

'The chopper has landed, let me go and receive Mr Damnky.'

'Okay, sir.'

*****

'Good afternoon, sir.'

'Where is the car? It's so hot here.'

'Sir, the car is waiting for you, please come this way.'

'Let's move fast, Chandiyak.'

'This way, sir.'

'Hmm.'

*****

'Good afternoon, sir.'

'Take us to the podium.'

'Sure, sir.'

'I am going with the boss, you guys follow our car.'

'Yes, sir.'

*****

'Chandiyak, we are getting late, get into the car.'

'Yes, sir.'

'So what is the status?'

'Sir, we have gathered a crowd of 1.5 lac people.'

'*Hmmm.* That's impressive. How much did it cost us?'

'Sir, it's per person food, conveyance and 500 Grandaes.'

'What is the total spending on these people?'

'Around 12 crore Grandaes.'

'Are you kidding? I guess last time it was only 7 crore Grandaes. Why it is so expensive this time?'

'Nowadays lots of parties are spending huge amount of money on bringing the people to their rallies and speeches than what they used to spend earlier. This is one of the main reasons that there has been surge in the cost this time as we have to match our competitors' rates. Secondly, there is an increase in food and conveyance prices as well. Earlier the cost was not that high but now it has increased substantially.'

'*Hmmm.*'

'Sir, we have also brought some people for seven hundred grandaes, food and conveyance.'

'What for?'

'The main job of these guys shall be to chant our party's and your name. This shall bring more publicity to us.'

'How many of them have you brought for this job?'

'Fifteen thousand people.'

'The idea is good but it's very expensive.'

'Sir, last time the opposition party has brought ten thousand people for this job and I heard that these guys have done a great job for them. That is the reason why I brought fifteen thousand people for this job.'

'*Hmmm.* Okay, I can understand, if our competitors are doing this then we can't lag behind.'

'Yes, sir.'

'So how are the security arrangements?'

'We have hired the best people for the business.'

'I hope I shall be able to finish my speech within forty-five minutes and then I shall leave for Goodsdaeae.'

'Okay, sir.'

'By any chance, do you know by how many minutes I am late for this speech?'

'Well, I have not counted that, sir.'

'But still do you have any idea?'

'Roughly four hours.'

'Not bad. I guess last time I was late by seven hours so I am improving.'

'Sir, last time where you have given speech was a very remote location so that is the reason you were late.'

'Again, next week I have to visit Bundechuae.'

'Yes, sir.'

'So how much more time it's going to take to reach the podium?'

'We have reached, sir.'

'Stop the car then.'

'Sure, sir.'

*****

'Long live Mr Damnky! Long live Mr Damnky! Long live Mr Damnky!'

'*Hmmm.* Nice arrangements, Chandiyak.'

'It's my pleasure, sir.'

'Mr Damnky, what are your party's chances in this election?'

'Chandiyak, ask these media people not to ask any questions now. Let me first finish my speech.'

'Excuse me, friends. Mr Damky shall address you guys after his speech is over, so no questions now.'

'Mr Damnky, what are you plans for the poor people?'

'Chandiyak, which way do we have to go?'

'Sir, this way, please.'

*****

'Long live Mr Damnky! Long live Mr Damnky! Long live Mr Damnky!

'Ladies and gentlemen, we have our great leader Mr Damnky with us. Applause, please.'

'Long live Mr Damnky! Long live Mr Damnky! Long live Mr Damnky!'

'Ladies and gentlemen, now I request the young girl who has come from Vidhatis orphanage to give the flower bouquet to our beloved leader Mr Damnky.'

'Long live Mr Damnky! Long live Mr Damnky! Long live Mr Damnky!

'Applause, please.'

'Long live Mr Damnky! Long live Mr Damnky! Long live Mr Damnky!

'Ladies and Gentleman, as time is running short and Mr Damnky has some other gatherings to be addressed to, so without wasting much time I would like to request Mr Damnky to say a few words to all of us.'

'Long live Mr Damnky! Long live Mr Damnky! Long live Mr Damnky!'

'Good afternoon, my dear ladies and gentlemen.'

'Good afternoon. Good afternoon. Long live Mr Damnky! Long live Mr Damnky! Long live Mr Damnky!'

'I guess all is well.'

'All is well. All is well. Long live Mr Damnky! Long live Mr Damnky! Long live Mr Damnky!

First of all, I would like to thank all of you for coming here. I would also like to apologise for coming late. It's a great honour for me to say a few words in front of you. Guys, you all rock!'

'Long live Mr Damnky! Long live Mr Damnky! Long live Mr Damnky!'

'We all are already late so without wasting much time let me start.'

'Yuppies! Long live Mr Damnky! Long live Mr Damnky! Long live Mr Damnky!'

'My friends, this year has not been good for us. There has been severe drought in many parts of the nation. Many of our farmers and other brothers got severely affected by the drought. We have decided to supply food and other commodities from government owned Godowns to our brothers.'

'Great going. Long live Mr Damnky! Long live Mr Damnky! Long live Mr Damnky!'

'We shall do everything to help our brothers who have been affected because of the drought.'

'Long live Mr Damnky! Long live Mr Damnky! Long live Mr Damnky!'

'Friends, to improve the conditions of roads in our country we have planned to bring experts from Zeubikes. These experts shall study the situation of roads in our country and based on their reports and suggestion we shall move forward. We have already allotted funds and very soon we shall have state of the art roads in our country.'

'Long live Mr Damnky! Long live Mr Damnky! Long live Mr Damnky!

'Friends, we have planned to open four thousand schools for those children who can't afford studies. This shall help us to eradicate the illiteracy from our great nation. The illiteracy is eating our nation like a termite and we just can't see this happening. My dear people, these small children are the future of our nation and they can't be deprived of education.'

'Very well said! Long live Mr Damnky! Long live Mr Damnky! Long live Mr Damnky!'

'Ladies and gentlemen, nowadays many illegal vaccines and medicines are sold in the market. We came to know that a lot of kids are getting affected because of that. We have set up a committee to investigate this and anyone who is found guilty shall not be spared.'

'Long live Mr Damnky! Long live Mr Damnky! Long live Mr Damnky!

'Ladies and gentlemen, we have set up a special committee for investigating corruption cases. We have also set up a committee for investigating the black money issue.'

'Good step! Great going! Long live Mr Damnky! Long live Mr Damnky! Long live Mr Damnky!'

'Friends, this widespread insect named corruption is making our nation hallow. We can't let this happen. Very soon you shall be seeing the results from the committee.'

'Long live Mr Damnky! Long live Mr Damnky! Long live Mr Damnky!'

'Friends, very soon we shall bring all the black money back to our nation. The committee is working day in and day out towards it. The money shall be used for the development of AlphaLand.'

'Long live Mr Damnky! Long live Mr Damnky! Long live Mr Damnky!'

'There are still lots of facilities to be given in to remote and other places. Friends, in the future no one shall be deprived of food, electricity, house, education, jobs, and other necessary things in AlphaLand.'

'Long live Mr Damnky! Long live Mr Damnky! Long live Mr Damnky!'

'No, friends, it's not long live Mr Damnky. It is long live AlphaLand! Long live AlphaLand! Come on, say with me, long live AlphaLand! Long live AlphaLand!'

'Yuppieee! Long live AlphaLand! Long live AlphaLand! Long live Mr Damnky! Long live Mr Damnky! Long live Mr Damnky!'

*****

'Excuse me, sir.'

'What the hell?'

'Sir, an accident took place.'

'So what?'

'Sir, the media is trying to make a huge issue out of it.'

'The media has no other work. You carry on with your work.'

'Sir, this is really a serious issue.'

'Tell me fast I don't have time.'

'Some people were chanting our party slogans and were chasing Mr Damnky's car from the helipad.'

'So?'

'They ran through an electric pole.'

'So?'

'Sir, two people have died and five got severely injured. The media is making a huge issue out of it.'

'But how did it happen?'

'Sir, they were carrying our party flags on iron rods.'

'What the hell. Who asked them to carry iron rods? Why didn't they carry the flags on wooden sticks? Who the hell has given them the instructions?'

'Sir, we are investigating on that.'

'Find it out soon.'

'Yes, sir.'

'I guess we paid these guys seven hundred Grandaes, food, and conveyance?'

'Yes, sir.'

'What a waste of money. Where did we find these morons? Didn't they know that they should have not carried iron rods and ran through electric poles? I want to know each and every detail on this.'

'Sure, sir.'

'You can leave now and get on with your work. I will inform Mr Damnky.'

'Okay, sir.'

*****

'My dear people, this year . . .'

'Excuse me, sir.'

'Yes.'

'Something very urgent, sir.'

'What the hell . . .'

'I am sorry, sir, but it is really urgent.'

'I beg your pardon, my dear people, but please excuse me for a second. Something very urgent has cropped up.'

'I am sorry, sir. I had to interrupt you in between but this is very urgent.'

'Mr Udasie, can you address the people for a second. I will be just back.'

'Sure, sir.'

'What the hell, Chandiyak! Can't you wait for a while? What was so urgent that you had to stop me in between?'

'I am sorry, sir, but something important has come up.'

*****

'Ladies and gentleman, hope you all are having a great time.'

'Yuppies!'

'Because of some very important matter, Mr Damnky had to take a break from his speech but he shall be back very soon. Sorry for the inconvenience.'

'Long live Mr Damnky! Long live Mr Damnky! Long live Mr Damnky!'

*****

'Will you tell me what the urgency is?'

'Some people were chasing our car from the helipad and they met with an accident.'

'So what? It happens.'

'The media is trying to make a big issue out of it.'

'What?'

'Yes, we have to do something.'

'How did this happen?'

'They were carrying our party flags on iron rods and were chanting our party slogan when they met with the accident. Two people died on the spot and five are severely injured.'

'Gosh, and you must have paid them for running behind our car?'

'Yes, sir. Seven hundred Grandaes, food, and conveyance.'

'Oh great, Mr Chandiyak! You are proving your worth for every bit of penny that I have invested on you.'

'I am sorry, sir.'

'You swine! You have hired idiots who can't even do their jobs properly. You have hired morons who can't even monitor things properly!'

'I am sorry, sir.'

'What sorry? Don't you do proper ground work before you hire people?'

'I am sorry, sir, but everything was going smoothly before this incident happened.'

'Let me see what I can do about these media guys.'

'Okay, sir.'

'What investigation are you doing?'

'The boys are doing thorough investigation. We shall have something concrete in sometime.'

'I want each and every piece of information.'

'Sure, sir.'

*****

'Mr Udasie, I am on.'

'Sure, sir. My dear ladies and gentlemen our great leader, Mr Damnky, is back.'

'Yuippeee! Hurraaaaaa! Long live Mr Damnky! Long live Mr Damnky! Long live Mr Damnky!'

'My dear people, please accept my apologies for leaving the speech in between. Something very urgent has come up so that is the reason I had to take break from my speech. I am sorry for the inconvenience caused.'

'No problems. No problems. Long live Mr Damnky! Long live Mr Damnky! Long live Mr Damnky!'

'People, before I begin my speech again let me first tell you about the incident that has just happened and because of which I had to stop my speech in between. Do you guys want to know about it?'

'Yes, please tell us. Please tell us.'

'Some people who are our die hard supporters and who have firm belief in our party's core values have met with an accident. They were chanting our party slogans and were carrying our party flags before they ran through an electric pole. Two of them have died on the spot and five are seriously injured. This is really very sad news. My dear people, our party has decided to give five lacs Grandaes to each of the deceased family and two lacs Grandaes to each of the injured family. Our party has decided to take care of the families of the victims. We can't leave our people suffering. We are always there for them.'

'Long live Mr Damnky! Long live Mr Damnky! Long live Mr Damnky!'

'Okay, people. Allow me to start my speech again.'

'Long live Mr Damnky! Long live Mr Damnky! Long live Mr Damnky!'

'People, this has been a year of lots of ups and downs. There has been steep increase in fuel and commodity prices but we have rolled back the prices now by 15 per cent. It has been a tough decision for us but we can't put the burden on common man and thus we have rolled back the prices.'

'Long live Mr Damnky! Long live Mr Damnky! Long live Mr Damnky!'

'Ladies and gentlemen, this is your party, it exists today because of you all and it is nothing without you. The party gives its blood and sweat to deliver the promises that it has committed to you. The party's main agenda is always to fulfil your wishes and expectations.'

'Long live Mr Damnky! Long live Mr Damnky! Long live Mr Damnky!'

'Today, the way you all have come shows the faith that you have on us. The party can never forget this. I would like to request you all to come forward and vote for us. People, the victory of this party is the victory of you all.'

'Long live Mr Damnky! Long live Mr Damnky! Long live Mr Damnky!'

'This party shall give you whatever you desire, you dream, and you cherish for. This is the people's party.'

'Long live Mr Damnky! Long live Mr Damnky! Long live Mr Damnky!'

'Thank you, my dear ladies and gentlemen. Now with your permission, I shall take a leave and promise to return very soon. Long live people! Long live AlphaLand!'

'Long live Mr Damnky! Long live Mr Damnky! Long live Mr Damnky!'

'People, hope you have enjoyed the afternoon. Now our leader shall take a leave from us with a promise to return very soon.'

'Long live Mr Damnky! Long live Mr Damnky! Long live Mr Damnky!'

'Applause, please.'

'Long live Mr Damnky! Long live Mr Damnky! Long live Mr Damnky!'

*****

'Mr Damnky, what is your party planning to do for the rising unemployment issues?'

'No questions please, Mr Damnky has to rush for another meeting.'

'Mr Damnki, what do you have to say on the rising scams and corruption?'

'People, very soon we shall have a press conference wherein all your questions shall be answered.'

'Mr Damnky! Mr Damnky!'

'Chandiyak, let's go.'

'Sure, sir.'

'I hope you have done all the necessary arrangements as per my likings.'

'Of course, sir.'

'How far is Goodsdaeae?'

'Hardly twenty minutes, sir.'

'Hmmm.'

'Sir, today your speech was really good.'

'Hmmm.'

'This shall give a good coverage to our party.'

'Hmmm.'

'I was really scared about the electric pole incident. Media people were making a lot of hue and cry about it. But you have made a great announcement for the victims, the entire AlphaLand must have watched that. Now this shall be in our favour.'

'See, I had to make that announcement or else the media would have dragged the issue like anything. This election is important for us and we can't afford to lose it by any reason. Whatever promise we have to make let's make it or else we can't win the faith of the people. Don't worry about fulfilling them, in the past we made so many promises but we haven't fulfilled most of them. I guess most of the time we have fulfilled only 10 per cent of the promises that we have made.'

'Yes, sir.'

'See, today also whatever promises we have made we are not going to fulfil all of them. We have to do some brain storming on what we have to fulfil rather than focusing on each and everything. Once the elections are over then who cares what we have committed.'

'Yes, sir.'

'So what is the status of the interrogation about the electric pole incident?'

'We are almost through and in a couple of hours I shall present you the report.'

'Ensure that whosoever has given the instruction to carry iron rod is not to be spared. We have invested so much of money for this event, the entire nation was watching and we don't want this kind of crap to ruin all this.'

'Sir, I shall see to it that this kind of incident doesn't repeat.'

'So how much more time?'

'We are almost there.'

#####

'Sands! Sands! Wake up! What you are you thinking again?'

'What?'

'In which world were you? I was yelling at top of my lungs, what were you thinking about?'

'Well nothing.'

'The speech is almost over and we have to leave.'

*****

'My dear ladies and gents, we are done with our presentations. We shall be floating the links for the opinion poll and details of the work done by us very soon on the website. If you feel that we have been worth of the vote given by you then please elect us again and I promise that we shall not let you down, bye for now. 'Hip! Hip! Hurray! Hip! Hip! Hurray!' Long live AlphaLand! Long live AlphaLand!'

'Hall, you rock! Hall, you are the gem! Long live Hall! Long live Hall!

*****

'Sands, let's move now.'

'Okay.'

'So how did you like it though? I guess for a while you were in some other world.'

'Jeans, let me tell you I have never seen or heard a politician coming like a rock star and the people just go crazy about him. This was truly beyond my imaginations.'

'This is how our leaders are. They are a true gem.'

'I have seen there was lot of adulation for your leader.'

'Yup!'

'So what's next?'

'Let's hurry up, we have to go somewhere else.'

'Where are we going now? I am feeling hungry so let's have food first.'

'Okies, let's go for lunch then and after that we shall proceed further.'

'Okay.'

Chapter Six

BadaeMehfile

'Good afternoon, madamae. Good afternoon, sirae.'

'Good afternoon. Take us to Dinofigae Street.'

'Yes, madamae.'

'Is Dinofigae Street famous for food?'

'Almost all the places in AlphaLand are famous for food.'

'Yeah, you told me that.'

'So how is your experience so far in AlphaLand?'

'Madamae, would you like to listen to some music?'

'No, it's okay.'

'It's a new track, madamae.'

'Are you talking about *You Know Who Shall?*'

'You are right, madamae.'

'What is this new track, Jeans?'

'It's a worldwide hit and around one billion copies are already sold out.'

'My goodness!'

'The track is dedicated to old people who are left alone in their old age.'

'Okay.'

'I guess this track came just one month back and within a month it has gained so much of popularity.'

'That's quite impressive.'

'Hey, we have reached Dinofigae Street, can you stop the cab there?'

'Sure, madamae.'

'Thanks!'

'Welcome, madamae. Welcome, sirae.'

'Come, Sands, let's go to that restaurant "Buzurge Khwaishea".'

'This restaurant looks fabulous. It's in milky white colour.'

'This is one of the oldest restaurants in AlphaLand.'

'Okay.'

*****

'Good afternoon, madamae. Good afternoon, sirae.'

'Good afternoon.'

'How may I help you?'

'We need seats for two people.'

'My pleasure, madamae. Please come this way.'

'Actually, we need a seat where we can have a good view.'

'Sure, madamae, as you wish.'

'Thanks.'

'Here is the seat, madamae, as per your wish. Please enjoy your lunch.'

'Thanks.'

'My pleasure, madamae.'

'The ambience of the restaurant is quite good, Jeans.'

'It's all made up of wood.'

'Amazing!'

'Yeah, and look at the view, it's awesome!'

'I relish food with mountain view.'

'So do I, Sands.'

'So what are we ordering then? For me anything will do, I shall go with you.'

'Okay, then let me order something delicious for both of us.'

'Sounds good.'

'Excuse me, please.'

'Yes, madamae.'

'Please get two cumbeyo, one daikeis, and five chalabeloos.'

'Sure and anything to drink, madamae?'

'Sands, do you care to have some drinks?'

'No, thanks.'

'That would be all.'

'Sure, madamae.'

'So, Sands, just taste the food and you shall never forget this place.'

'I have not even heard the name of the food that you have ordered.'

'They are all famous here.'

'But the names are so different.'

'You may have not heard the name but just taste them then you will realize what I was trying to say.'

'Okay, let's see.'

'Sure.'

'Hmmm.'

'So, Sands, how is your experience in AlphaLand till now? I hope you are enjoying here.'

'Actually, I am confused.'

'Confused but why?'

'I mean, you are saying this is AlphaLand but actual AlphaLand is the place from where I came. AlphaLand is not that clean, the leaders are not that good, corruption is quite rampant, every other day there is a crime and scam and the list goes on and on and on. How can the same country have two different images? There is something wrong, whatever you have shown is just like seeing dream in reality. This can't happen in AlphaLand. This country can't be AlphaLand.'

'Sands, you have gone mad. I don't understand what you want to say.'

'Jeans, what I want to say is . . .'

'Here comes the food, let's have it, I am really feeling hungry.'

'Jeans, I was trying to say something.'

'Can we discuss that later? I am really feeling hungry so let's have food now?'

'Okay, but you cannot avoid my questions.'

'I am not avoiding your questions. What I am saying is let's discuss it after having food.'

'Okay.'

'Sands, mix cumbeyo with daikeis and eat it first and then have chalabeloos.'

'Okay, let me try.'

'You shall love it.'

'*Hmmm.* It tastes good.'

'I told you it shall taste good.'

'Yeah, seems to be.'

'Enjoy the food, Sands.'

'Yup.'

'Excuse me, madamae.'

'Yes?'

'Would you like to have anything else?'

'Ah, nothing else right now. If we require anything then we shall let you know.'

'Sure, madamae.'

'Sands, I guess we should finish our lunch quickly or else we shall be late.'

'Can't we go tomorrow? I don't want to leave this place right now, this place is out of world.'

'I know this place is lovely and lives up to its reputation but we can come here again.'

'Hmmm.'

'Would you like to have anything in the desserts?'

'I don't think I have enough space left in my stomach now.'

'Okay then, let's finish quickly.'

'Yup!'

*****

'Sands, it's very difficult to walk after having heavy food.'

'I agree with you, Jeans. So are we taking a cab?'

'Of course yes.'

*****

'Good afternoon, madamae. Good afternoon, sirae.'

'Good afternoon, can you take us to BadaeMehfile, please?'

'Okay, madamae.'

'What is this BadaeMehfile?'

'You shall find it soon.'

'Every time you are having this habit of maintaining secrecy.'

'It has its own fun.'

'I know how much fun it has. It increases the curiosity like anything.'

'Don't get frustrated.'

'I am not but every time you keep a secret, there is no fun at all.'

'Oh, come on, Sands, it's a matter of a few minutes.'

'Madamae, is sirae new to AlphaLand?'

'Yes, but why are you asking this?'

'I have asked this because he doesn't know about BadaeMehfile. I haven't met an AlphaLandite who doesn't know about BadaeMehfile.'

'He is our guest in AlphaLand.'

'Okay, that's great. Have a nice stay here, sirae.'

'Yeah, thanks.'

'I guess we have reached BadaeMehfile, can you stop that side?'

'Sure, madamae.'

'Thanks.'

'Have a nice day, madamae. Have a nice day, sirae.'

'Yeah, you too, have a nice day.'

'Sure, madamae.'

*****

'So, Jeans, where is your surprise?'

'Have some patience, Sands.'

'I hope I shall not have to take another birth to see your prestigious BadaeMehfile.'

'Let's cross the small lane there.'

'Where are you taking me?'

'Can we walk through the small lane, please?

'Yeah.'

'Good.'

'We have to walk how far?'

'Only for a few seconds.'

'Hmmm.'

'So, Sands, here we are.'

'Wow! What a place, Jeans!'

'So, Sands, let me have the honour to show you the BadeaMehfile.'

'Oh my goodness! This building looks dazzling!'

'Sands, this is one of the most cherished buildings of AlphaLand.'

'I guess it's completely made up of glass.'

'Well, it's not a glass structure but something very similar to it. One can just jump, hit, and pass through it but it doesn't break.'

'What?'

'You can see there are no doors to enter this building. To get inside one has to pass through it.'

'How can one pass through it? If one tries to pass then either the glass shall break or the person shall get wounded. I have never seen or heard anything of this kind before.'

'Sands, if you can't believe me then just look at that guy. See how he is entering the building.'

'Oh my goodness! How can he enter like that? The glass didn't break at all.'

'Yes, Sands, that is what I was trying to tell you.'

'How is it possible?'

'The material used to make this structure is of a very special quality. It took so many years of research and development to make this building.'

'But how does it work?'

'The building has special sensors. When the person comes near to it then the sensors read the body temperature and because of which it melts and softens. The person can then easily pass through it and once the person passes through it then again it comes back to its normal position.'

'You want to say that our body temperature is the key to enter the building?'

'You can interpret it like that.'

'*Hmmm.* That sounds different. Jeans, what is that?'

'It's the mascot called Woolwo.'

'Okay.'

*****

'Good afternoon, madamae. Good afternoon, sirae.'

'Good afternoon, Woolwo.'

'Welcome to BadeaMehfile.'

'Thanks.'

'Cheers!'

'Woolwo, he is our guest in AlphaLand.'

'Ooye! That's great. Sirae, I hope you are enjoying yourself and I wish for your pleasant stay at AlphaLand.'

'Woolwo, why are you wearing a yellow shirt and red trousers today?'

'Today is the friendship day, madamae.'

'How can I forget that? Happy friendship day, Woolwo!'

'Happy friendship day, madamae. Happy friendship day, sirae.'

'Thanks, Woolwo. Come, Sands, let's go inside.'

'Okay.'

'Are you seeing the screen there?'

'Yes.'

'We have to go at the screen and say our name and address. The screen captures our photo and maps our name and address against it. Once it is done then we can enter inside.'

'Okay.'

'I will begin and you follow me.'

'I hope I shall be able to enter the building safely.'

'Don't worry, Sands, you shall be fine.'

'Okay.'

'You have to just follow me.'

*****

'Good afternoon, madamae.'

'Good afternoon.'

'Your name, please?'

'Jeena.'

'Your address, please?'

'002 Kulepobea, Trtudivo, Zulebiea-3rt56.'

'Thanks for the information, madamae. You can enter inside.'

'Thanks. Sands, follow me.'

'Good afternoon, sirae.'

'Good afternoon.'

'Your name, please?'

'Sandeep.'

'Your address, please?

'321 AlphoCubae, Cubinaoes- 4er67.'

'Thanks for the information, sirae. You can enter inside.'

'I hope I shall be able to enter safely.'

'Sirae, you can enter inside.'

'Excuse me, mate, the machine is asking you to enter inside the building.'

'Sorry, mate, I was just trying to figure out to how to enter inside.'

'Ah, don't worry at all, just pass through it.'

'I hope I will not get hurt.'

'Not at all, mate.'

'Okay, let me try. Mom, please save me.'

'Go mate, don't worry.'

'I am coming, please save me.'

'Sands, are you okay?'

'Oh my goodness! I am safe. I just can't believe it!'

'Yeah, you're safe, Sands.'

'But how is it possible? How could I enter through the frame without breaking it?'

'Body temperature, Sands, you remember?'

'Yeah body temperature, the key to enter the building.'

'Sands, we can use any of the cars available that side to travel inside the BadaeMehfile.'

'Why do we need car?'

'Sands, the entire BadaeMehfile is spread across 3,500 acres of land so we will have to use a car.'

'That's quite huge.'

'So let's take the pink car, it looks good.'

'As you say.'

'Here we go for a spin.'

'Jeans, I am not finding a steering in the car?'

'Sands, when we step in the car, then we have to say the location's name and the car starts moving on its own because of our body weight.

'That means the more the weight the faster the car moves?'

'No, it's not like that. The minimum weight should be 48 kilograms and maximum should be 400 kilograms or six people, whichever is more. The car moves at a speed of 25 kph and it is constant.'

'Don't we have to give any direction to the car?'

'No, we don't have to give any direction, the car moves on its own and it knows all the directions.'

'How does it stop then?'

'Once the car reaches the location it stops on its own.'

'That means all the locations and directions are mapped in it?'

'Yup!'

'It's a cool car!'

'Yeah.'

'Jeans, BadaeMehfile looks like a very big place with lots of sections, what are these sections like?'

'There are various sections like the infrastructure section which has the details of road, air, and water connectivities. Similarly, education section has details of schools and colleges. Then there are other sections like fuel section, justice section, scam and scandals section, GDP section, tax section, employment section, social economic classification section, global section, and the list goes on and on and on.'

'What is there in the global section?'

'The global section gives comparison details of AlphaLand with other countries.'

'That sounds interesting. Jeans, there are televisions, indicators, and other displays at each section. What are these for?'

'Yeah, Sands, each section has televisions and other displays which show updates pertaining to that particular section. At each section you will also find government representative.'

'What is the role of these representatives?'

'These representatives listen to the query and concerns of the people and they put them before the government. They also share with the people about new initiatives taken by the government and the action plan that the government shall be taking to resolve the issues raised by the people.'

'That sounds good.'

'AlphaLand is one of the few countries in the world that has this type of facilities available for its citizens. AlphaLand gives its countrymen complete transparency and people can actually see what is happening around the country.'

'Okay.'

'Let me take you to the demographics, geographic, and history section.'

'Okay.'

'Get into the car.'

'Sure.'

'Ithihasae, Chetrae, and Loggae of issae Desae.'

'What did you say?'

'Loggae of issae Desae is for Demographics, Chetrae is for Geographic and Ithihasae is for History.'

'The name is very unique.'

'Yup.'

'It feels good in this car.'

'Haaaa.'

'Why did the car stop suddenly?'

'The section has come so we have to get down now.'

'Okay.'

'Let's first see the Ithihasae.'

'Sure!'

'The history of AlphaLand goes way back to thousands of years. Initially people from gold community settled down here and after that people from other communities like fishing came and settled here. Things were quite good for many years but after that AlphaLand was looted by

Dacoits, army men, kings, and rulers of other nations. The nation once known for its prosperity and wealth was turned into rubbles. People became destitute and died of hunger. They became slaves in their own country for more than 300 years.'

'That sounds very sad.'

'Sands, it is said that once a very great monk visited this place before any of the communities settled here and he made certain predictions about this place. He said that this nation is destined to be the richest, most desired, and powerful nation of the world. But there shall be many years of turbulence in between and once that phase is gone then nobody can stop this nation from becoming the greatest nation in the world.'

'Sounds quite interesting.'

'The great monk also said that this place shall be surrounded by rivers, lakes, and seas. This nation will have as many friends and as many enemies but it shall be so self-sustained and secured that no one can combat it.'

'Okay.'

'So after 300 odd years of slavery the people of this nation stood together and fought against the people who ruled them. It is said that the rulers were quite powerful and dangerous but nothing stopped the people of AlphaLand to fight against them. It was a matter of pride, values, and want. These great men fought for more than fifteen years to free AlphaLand from clutches of those wolves who were here for more than 300 years.'

'Quite impressive.'

'It is said that there were some thirty people who were quite instrumental in uniting and motivating the people of AlphaLand. These guys were fearless and they made strategies that could even shock the best of warfare strategists of the world.'

'Hmmm.'

'AlphaLand is now free for more than seventy-four years and next month is the 75th anniversary. You should just see the way the independence celebrations happen. It's the best day for each and every AlphaLandite.'

'Okay.'

'Sands, we all are proud of those great people who sacrificed their life for the independence of AlphaLand. They lost their lives for a cause which was to free AlphaLand and make it an independent nation. Today, we all are experiencing this beautiful life and seeing this beautiful nation because those great martyrs dared to fight those bloody wolves and threw them out.'

'That's great!'

'Sands, here you can find details about popular personalities, leaders, freedom fighters, monuments, heritage properties, important places, currencies, developed areas of the past and their current status, kings and their kingdoms, civilization, and the list goes on and on and on.'

'Okay.'

'Let's see the Chetrae.'

'Sure.'

'AlphaLand is divided into thirty-five parts and each part is a state. These states are further classified under five zones which is EKae, Doae, Teenae, Chaarae, and Paanchae. The capital city of Alpha Land is Endraepristaeae.'

'Okay.'

'Here we can see the geographical details about the formation of AlphaLand.'

'Okay.'

'Sands, AlphaLand is surrounded by four oceans. In the south it is surrounded by the great Southsamudrae, in the east by the great Eastsamudrae, the west by the great Westsamudrae, and in the north by the great Northsamudrae.'

'Okay.'

'These four seas are the major seas of the world and as they surround this country so that is the reason the name AlphaIsland came out and later changed to AlphaLand.'

'I know this.'

'How do you know this? Oh, I guess you may have studied it somewhere.'

'Nothing, please carry on.'

'AlphaLand has always been an important commercial centre as it has got good sea connectivity with other countries. AlphaLand has got twelve neighbouring countries and with all it is connected through sea.'

'Okay.'

'AlphaLand has got thirty-five rivers and out of which in twelve rivers the gold is found in abundance.'

'What?'

'AlphaLand has the world's largest gold, mineral, uranium, and coal mines. All these mines are protected through robust security mechanisms.'

'Okay.'

'These mines are allotted to both private and government companies based on the merit and if anyone is found involved in any illegal activity then that person or entity is not spared.'

'Okay.'

'Details about coastlines, rivers, species, deserts, forests, rainfalls, and other geographical aspects are also available. If you wish then you can have a look.'

'I guess I shall read it later.'

'Okay.'

'Let's see the demographics.'

'Okay.'

'With 99 crores residents reported in the 2012 provisional census, AlphaLand is one of the world's most populous country- the human sex ratio is 1,001 females per 1,000 males and the median age is 27 years.'

'Okay.'

'All the people in AlphaLand speak Alphahindae and it is the national language. English language is also widely spoken and is also used in education, business, administration, and for other purposes.'

'Okay.'

'Sands, despite having so many religions and diversity there is still unity in AlphaLand which cannot be broken. No one tries to politicize these things as each and every individual in AlphaLand have moral values which is deeply rooted. Each and every citizen of AlphaLand has the moral responsibility to spread harmony and bondness within AlphaLand.'

'Okay.'

'Sands, anyone found spreading disharmony is not spared.'

'Okay.'

'Patriotism is a very important thing in AlphaLand. After a child is born he or she is nurtured about patriotism and harmony. The child is taught that country comes first and nothing is more valuable than the country.'

'Okay.'

'Each and every person of AlphaLand spends four years in the service of the country and countrymen. They join defense or some social service organizations, but two and a half years of defense service is compulsory. Every morning, each and every home sings the national anthem before commencing on their daily job.'

'That sounds great. This gives energy. It pumps the adrenaline and makes a person feel that he is at the top of the world. He or she feels nothing is impossible and that makes the day of the person.'

'Okay.'

'If you have any questions then you can ask the government representative.'

'No, I don't have any.'

'Okay then, let me take you to the infrastructure section.'

'Sure.'

'Budachae.'

'Wow, Jeans! The moment you said the name the car has started moving in other direction.'

'Yes, it is now moving towards infra section now.'

'Hmmm.'

'I hope you liked the Ithihasae, Chetrae, and Loggae of issae Desae section.'

'It was okay.'

'I hope you are enjoying here.'

'Yeah, this place looks good.'

'Sands, we have reached the infra section. Let's get down here.'

'Sure.'

'Come, let's go inside.'

'Okay.'

'Sands, here you shall find the updates on road, SuperTrans network, flyovers, electricity, etcetera, etcetera.'

'Hmmm.'

'Let me take you to the updates on road status.'

'Okay.'

'Concrete Roads: 99 per cent (53.5 Lacs Miles). Bitumen Road: 1 per cent (0.5 Lacs Miles).'

'Jeans, I guess the majority of the roads in AlphaLand are made up of concrete.'

'Yup. Now let's see the lanes specifications.'

'Okay.'

'. . . 18 Lanes- 14 Lacs Miles, 16 lanes- 2 lacs mile 12 Lanes – 14 Lacs Miles, 10 Lanes – 8 lacs miles, 8 Lanes – 8 lacs miles, 6 Lanes – 8 Lacs miles.'

'The roads are bigger and wider.'

'Sands, people in AlphaLand prefer wider roads and smooth drive.'

'Okay.'

'Status of connectivity: all Tier 1 cities are connected with 16 and 18 -lane roads, Tier 1 and Tier 2 cities are connected with 12-lane roads, all the Tier 2 cities are connected with 12-lane roads and all the other places getting converted to 12-lane roads from 10-, 8-, and 6-lane roads.'

'The connectivity looks quite great.'

'Yup. Let's now see the major projects.'

'What are the projects like?'

'It's converting of the entire 16-lane to 18-lane roads. Sands, already 95 per cent of the work has been done in this area.'

'*Hmmm.* Looks like projects are going in full swing.'

'Yeah.'

'Jeans, what is the quality of the material used for making the roads?'

'Sands, lots of vehicle movements happen in AlphaLand on a daily basis. The roads in AlphaLand have to go with lots of different types of weather changes like in monsoons it rains quite heavily and during winters and summers it's quite cold and hot. Taking all these factors into consideration, the quality of materials used is quite good but still as a precaution the repair work happens once in every twenty years.'

'That means no repair works happen for twenty years.'

'Yeah, that's right.'

'Unbelievable!'

'Why are you saying so?'

'Well, very tough to believe?'

'Why?'

'Well nothing, let's move forward.'

'Okay, let's see the SuperTrans status: Maximum speed of the passenger SuperTrans for shorter distance is 550 miles per hour and for farther distance is 980 miles per hour and for freight SuperTrans is 910 miles per hour. Number of stations are twenty thousand across AlphaLand and all are high-tech stations with shopping malls, food joints, commercial spaces, offices, club/ recreation centres and so on and so forth.'

'Hmmm.'

'Come let's see electricity status.'

'Okay.'

'All the places in AlphaLand are connected with electricity and the electricity downtime is nil.'

'That means there is no place in AlphaLand without electricity?'

'That's true.'

'Unbelievable.'

'Now let's see the water status.'

'Okay.'

'All the places in AlphaLand are well supplied with drinking water and water used for other purposes. Water supply is done 24/ 7 across AlphaLand without any downtime.'

'Sounds very amazing.'

'Sands, water is a basic necessity and that is the reason it is given top priority.'

'Okay.'

'Let's see other updates.'

'Like?'

'Sands, let's now see the details of bridges, flyovers, sea links, sky walks, and super sky walks.'

'Okay.'

'Let's see the details of bridges and flyovers. All the conjunction points and major locations are connected with bridges and flyovers.'

'Okay.'

'All bridges and flyovers are of 12 lanes.'

'*Hmmm.*'

'Next is the Sea Links.'

'Okay.'

'Sea and rivers across AlphaLand are connected with 12-lane sea links.'

'Okay.'

'Sands, all the public places are connected with sky walks and super sky walks.'

'Jeans, what's the difference between sky walks and super sky walks?'

'In super sky walks there are travelators and one can move faster by using them but in sky walks there are no travelators.'

'By travelators do you mean like the ones in airports?'

'Yeah, right.'

'*Hmmm.*'

'Sands, let's see the air connectivity details.'

'Can I see this later?'

'Why are you finding this boring?'

'No, it's not boring but I just wanted to see other sections.'

'Okay, no probs but seeing air connectivity details shall not take much time. Let's see it fast.'

'Okay.'

'All Tier1, Tier2, Tier3, Tier4 places are connected with each other by high speed Jumboea jet air network.'

'What is this High Speed Jumboea Jet air network?'

'Well it can travel in fogs, snow, rain, windy, and stormy conditions without any hindrance and signal issues. Even if fuel is finished then also it can carry the passengers safely to the destination. Its speed is 3,000 miles per hour. It is resistant to fire, bomb, and any other stuff that can create havoc.'

'It might be expensive?'

'Yes, you are right, it's expensive. It took lots of years for the scientists to develop this amazing stuff.'

'Hmmm.'

'Well there are lots of other updates that can be seen but as you want to go to the other section, so let's move. Before moving, if you have any questions then you can ask the government representative.'

'Well, I don't have any questions'

'Okies, then let's go to the education section.'

'Okay.'

'Come get into the car.'

'Yup!'

'Vidyae.'

'Jeans, I have a question.'

'But you said you didn't have any questions.'

'Well it's not related to infra section. It's a generic one.'

'What is it?'

'Just wanted to know how it is possible for all people to visit this place?'

'Sands, for seeing this place you don't have to visit here.'

'But we have visited here, right?'

'We have visited here because I wanted to show this place to you. But there is also another way to see this place.'

'What is that?'

'One can visit this place through an online portal.'

'How is that possible?'

'The government has given each individual a unique ID. By using the ID the person can login to the website and visit the place.'

'How does it work?'

'The entire thing works on 3D technology. When the person logs in the website then that person's animated figure or cartoon enters into 3D view of the BadeaMehfile. It's just like how we are moving now, the same thing happens in the portal. All the sections can be seen, the person can travel in the car. Everything that we are doing now can be done in the portal.'

'This sounds very different. That means people have to be just online to visit to BadeaMehfile?'

'Yup.'

'That's interesting.'

'Sands, we are now at the education section.'

'Okay.'

'Let's go inside then.'

'Jeena, this place just looks like a temple.'

'Yeah, you are right, this place looks like a temple. In AlphaLand we treat the place where education is provided like a temple.'

'Hmmm.'

'You can see there are different subsections.'

'What are they for?'

'They provide updates about schools, colleges, etcetera.'

'Let's first see the updates related to schools.'

'Okay.'

'Schools have classes from 1 to 12th std and all the schools are equipped with modern amenities.'

'What do you mean by modern amenities?'

'Well these schools have computer labs, libraries, games, theatres, gymnasiums, football grounds, tennis courts, cricket clubs, ballrooms, music, arts, dance rooms, canteens, movie halls, and other world class facilities. The faculties of these schools are renowned and these schools have tie up with colleges and universities within AlphaLand and other countries.'

'How many of these kinds of schools are there in AlphaLand?'

'There are 6,500,000.'

'That is quite a huge number.'

'It's all as per the government's plan.'

'Hmmm.'

'Come, let's see the college section.'

'Okay.'

There are 'Colleges for graduation, PG, and doctorate. These colleges include general studies, arts, science, medical, computers, engineering, health care, and the list goes on and on and on.'

'Okay.'

'AlphaLand in total has 5,600,000 colleges with modern amenities.'

'I guess the meaning of modern amenities remains the same as what you have said for schools?'

'Yes, but one more thing that adds up to the list is the job. All the colleges provide jobs to the students who successfully complete the course. The jobs may be in the field of teaching, banking, nursing, law, medicine, engineering, science, and the list goes on and on and on.'

'Okay.'

'The college also funds the students or arranges the funds for those who want to be an entrepreneur provided the business plan shall be convincing and there shall be conviction.'

'Do the colleges have so much of funds with them to support someone who wishes to start his or her own venture?'

'Colleges in AlphaLand are government aided and also they have tie up with so many corporations, banks, industries, and other institutions. So arranging the funds are not that difficult.'

'Does the government believe in providing huge chunk of funds to the colleges?'

'Of course, yes. Every time in the budget the government allots good portion of money for this purpose.

The government of AlphaLand firmly believes that a strong nation can only be built if proper development of its people and students happen.'

'Okay.'

'So you see the literacy rate across AlphaLand is 100 per cent.'

'What is the definition of literacy?'

'See, the definition of literacy in AlphaLand is that the person should be able to write, read, understand, sign, and above all the person should be a graduate.'

'Are you sure?'

'Yes, but why are you asking like that?'

'No, nothing.'

'Well, you can also see the results of students across all the categories in AlphaLand.'

'Okay.'

'Do you want to see now?'

'Not right now.'

'Come, let's go to the lady out there. She is the representative.'

'But I don't have any question.'

'It's not going to take much time, come, let's go to her.'

'What for?'

*****

'Good afternoon, madamae. Good afternoon, sirae.'

'Hi, I am Jeena and he is Sands. He is our guest in AlphaLand.'

'Okay.'

'I have something to ask.'

'Yes, madamae.

'Well, can you elaborate on the projects in the pipeline at present?'

'Well there are loads of projects in the pipeline but the one that is on high priority is the collaboration of AlphaLand universities with colleges and universities of other countries.'

'But we are already having the collaborations then what are these new collaborations all about?'

'Well, most of our colleges and universities are having tie ups with colleges of other countries. But some of the colleges are still pending for the tie ups and the reason is that we could not find proper colleges for tie ups. The invites that we were getting from the colleges of other countries are below our benchmark. But this can't be a hindrance, so we are now in the process of looking for the good colleges for the tie ups.'

'But why is this project so important?'

'Sirae, this is important because our students can get more exposure and also other countries students can come and learn here. It is a transfer of knowledge amongst each other.'

'Okay.'

'Anything else that I can help you with?'

'Well thanks, you have been a great help.'

'Thank you, madamae. Thank you, sirae and have a great day!'

'You too, have a great day!'

'Sure, madamae.'

*****

'So, Sands, let's go to other sections?'

'Can we make our visit little bit shorter?'

'Why, what happened?'

'Well nothing, just wanted take some rest. I am feeling a little tired.'

'Sands, if you want then we can take a break.'

'No, it's okay.'

'Are you sure?'

'Yeah.'

'Okay, then let's go now to the employment section.'

'Sure.'

'Rojgarae.'

'Is that the name of the section?'

'Yes.'

'Again, a very different name.'

'The names are as per the nature of the section.'

'*Hmmm.*'

'So here comes the section. Let's go inside.'

'Sure.'

'In this section, the employment details pertaining to doctors, engineers, scientists, teachers, activists, policemen, defense personnel, artists, corporate people, and others are available.'

'Okay.'

'Sands, the unemployment status in AlphaLand is zero. This shows that all the ladies and gents are either employed or they are in some kind of business. The per capita income is 70 Lacs Grandaes per annum.'

'What?'

'Yes, that is one of the factors that shows that AlphaLand is a most developed nation.'

'But how authentic is the data?'

'Sands, once in every six months the survey happens. This survey is conducted by a third party or an agency which is chosen by the world organization after discussion with the government of AlphaLand. The third party conducts the survey through various mediums like physical survey, online survey, etcetera, etcetera.'

'What if someone is unemployed?'

'The chances of someone being unemployed is almost nil but even if someone is unemployed then that person can go online and raise the query. The government sees to it that within seven days he or she gets employed.'

'What if a person doesn't want to work?'

'Then no one can help that person.'

'Hmmm.'

'Sands, each and every citizen in AlphaLand is eligible for a government pension.'

'Okay.'

'Yup!'

'What kind of jobs do the people prefer?'

'Each and every individual has his or her own choice and they are encouraged for that. Details about each person and his or her jobs are available here.'

'How is that possible?'

'I have already told you about the unique number that is given while issuing the Viswasae card. The details are mapped against that number.'

'Okay.'

'Let's now go to the law and order, justice and crime section.'

'Can we see that some other day?'

'We shall not take much time.'

'Well I am feeling tired.'

'Then let's take a break at the snacks corner.'

'No, if we take a break then again it will be late. It's better to finish fast.'

'Okay then let's go to the law and order, justice and crime section.'

'Yeah.'

'I hope you are liking this place.'

'Well I am a little confused.'

'About what?'

'Nothing.'

'Sands, sometimes you behave very weird.'

'Why so?'

'One time you say that you are confused and when I ask you why you are confused then you say nothing.'

'Well, we will discuss it.'

'Let's discuss now.'

'Well, right now, let's get down from the car, I guess we have reached the law and order section.'

'Okay, but this discussion should happen.'

'Sure.'

'Okay, then let's see the section.'

'Yup!'

'Like all the other sections here also there are various subsections.'

'Okay.'

'Well the subsection called justice gives the details about the various courts, judges, lawyers, etcetera, etcetera. Basically, it gives details about the judicial system.'

'Okay.'

'There are courts in each of Tier1, 2, 3, and 4 cities and they are called City Courts. There are block courts at each block and one block contains twenty cities. The city courts report to the block courts. There are regional courts at each region and one region contains 100 blocks. The block courts report to the regional courts. The regional courts report to zonal courts. As I have earlier also said that AlphaLand is divide in 5 zones (EKae, Doae, Teenae, Chaarae, Paanchae), so there are five zonal courts and these zonal courts report to the country court and it is called Endraepristae Court, named after the capital city of AlphaLand.'

'Okay.'

'All these courts follow the hierarchy. The judicial system is independent and can't be influenced by anyone.'

'Are you sure?'

'Yes, 100 per cent, but why do you have to ask that?'

'Just out of curiosity.'

'If a city court gives some decision then other courts can't rule it out unless there are some serious challenges in the decision. If a judge has made a grave error then he or she is not spared.'

'Okay.'

'Sands, we also have consumer courts which is just inside the city courts. The hearing for it happens separately.'

'What is the average number of days taken to close a case?'

'The minimum is one day and the maximum is two months. On an average it takes twenty days to one month to close a case.'

'Are you serious?'

'Yes, I am. But why are you asking this?'

'It's hard to believe because cases run for years in the courts but still the verdict is not given.'

'Dude, this is AlphaLand and here it is not like that.'

'I would be really surprised if you are not wrong.'

'I don't know why you are trying to be so sarcastic.'

'Well, it was just a question, Jeans.'

'Anyways, let's now see the other details.'

'Okay.'

Here 'You can see the status of police stations and other institutions that are responsible for law and order in AlphaLand.'

'Okay.'

'There are citywise number of police stations and other institutions details available.'

There are how many institutions other than police stations for law and order?'

'Around sixty-seven law and order institutions in AlphaLand. The best part of all these institutions are that they're independent and cannot be influenced by anyone. No political party whether in ruling, opposition, or any other can pressurize or influence these bodies and their actions. In AlphaLand no one is above the law and the constitution and if anyone is found guilty then that person is not spared.'

'Okay.'

'Let's see the crime details.'

'Okay.'

'The crime issues are almost nil in AlphaLand. This includes all types of crimes like murder, rape, theft, suicides, domestic violence, cybercrime, and others.'

'Okay.'

'In AlphaLand, there is a saying that the people die only a natural death or death happens through some natural calamities. The law and order system is quite robust and there is no fatality because of crime.'

'Okay.'

'The terrorism activity is something that no one has heard of in AlphaLand for years now.'

'What do you mean by that?'

'Well, a major terrorist activity in AlphaLand happened fifty years back. That was not taken lightly, mass protests happened and people did not give up till the government and all the other party leaders across AlphaLand took a vow that a robust security system shall be made to counter terrorism. With lots of blood and sweat put into and with lots of efforts, a robust and very tight security system was developed and implemented.'

'Okay.'

'These security bodies work day in and day out for the security of AlphaLand. Those who are found guilty in terrorism are severely punished.'

'Okay.'

'The security of people is given the top priority and it can't be compromised for anything.'

'Okay.'

'Let's move now to other section.'

'Jeans, what's that section?'

'In that section the details of the culprits and Traitors of AlphaLand are available.'

Okay.

'You remember The Marro Kaminos Ko Dande Stan?'

'Yes, of course.'

'All the details about that are available in that section.'

'Okay.'

'So, Sands, let's go to the next section.'

'Let's see the other sections some other day as you know I am feeling a little tired so I want to take some rest.'

'Sands, I told you let's take a break at the snacks corner but you are not listening to me. I am still telling let's take a break and you shall feel good.'

'Jeans, why don't you understand that it's not necessary to see all the sections today itself, the rest of the sections can be seen some other day.'

'But only a few sections are left so why do you want to come for that some other day?'

'But I am not feeling good.'

'The time since we have come here, I am finding you a little weird.'

'What are you talking about?'

'Your body language says that you are a little uncomfortable here.'

'I don't know why you are talking like that. I am just feeling a little tired and that is the reason I said we can see the rest of the sections some other day.'

'I have told you we can take a break at the snacks corner.'

'I don't think that shall be a good idea.'

'At least we can try. Without trying how can you judge?'

'Okay, let's go.'

'Get in the car.'

'Okay.'

'Jalpanae.'

'Jeans, I never thought that you shall be thinking like this for me.'

'Well, whatever I felt I told you.'

'But I disagree with you.'

'Well we can talk about that.'

We have to.

'Come let's get down, we have reached the snacks corner.'

'Yeah.'

*****

'Good afternoon, madamae. Good afternoon, sirae.'

'Good afternoon.'

'Please make yourselves comfortable here.'

'Sure. Sands, I guess you will feel a little relaxed here.'

'How can I help you, madamae?'

'We will have Gumaeroyae.'

'What is Gumaeroyae?'

'Sands, it's a type of coffee and it's very famous.'

'Okay, then let's have that.'

'Please bring two Gumaeroyae for us.'

'Sure. Anything else, madamae?'

'Sands, would you like to have anything else?'

'Coffee shall be fine.'

'Okay, that's all.'

'Sure, madamae.'

*****

'Let's now discuss, Jeans.'

'What do you want to say?'

'Well, I am a little confused.'

'Confused about what?'

'I feel whatever you have shown is unreal.'

'What do you mean by that?'

'Whatever you have shown seems so perfect without any issues. This can't be real.'

'You are crazy.'

'AlphaLand is not like what you are showing me. I know AlphaLand than anybody else.'

'Have you gone nuts? How much do you know about AlphaLand? You have come here for the first time and you are talking as if this is your motherland. This is my motherland and I know about it than anybody else.'

'Excuse me, madamae, your coffee, please.'

'Thanks, if anything's needed then we shall call you.'

'Ok, madamae.'

'Jeans, I belong to AlphaLand and this is not the AlphaLand that I know. This is something else!'

'Sands, I guess you have lost your mind completely. Have some hot sips of coffee and you will regain your energy levels.'

'You are not trying to understand what I am saying.'

'Whatever you are trying to say doesn't make any sense.'

'But I am finding all of these things very flimsy.'

'Sands, let's not get involved in unnecessary discussions. Now you are saying this is not AlphaLand and after sometime you will be saying I am not Jeena and you are not Sands. It's all crap and idiotic.'

'But why you guys have stolen my country's name?'

'Why should we steal your country's name? Are you crazy?'

'Jeans, I told you my country's name is AlphaLAnd.'

'Shall I retaliate or shall I laugh at your thoughts? You are sounding like a kid. I suggest you relax for a while.'

'Okay, then let's not talk for a while. I need some silence.'

'Don't sound so rude, Sands.'

'Excuse me, madamae and sirae, sorry to bother you.'

'What happened?'

'Actually I forgot to bring webauiiersdae along with the coffee.'

'But we have not ordered that.'

'I know, madamae, but we are having an offer running now in which webauiiersdae is complimentary with Gumaeroyae.'

'Okay.'

'My apologies for not bringing it earlier.'

'It's okay.'

'Is sirae all right? He looks unwell.'

'He is okay. He wants to relax a bit.'

'We have restrooms available. If sirae wants then he can take a rest there.'

'Look, you smarty, I am all right. If you have served whatever you have brought then you can leave. If we need anything else then we shall let you know.'

'I am so sorry, sirae, my intensions were not to bother you. You please take care. Okay, madamae. Okay, sirae.'

'Sands, how can you talk to him like that? He was just trying to help you.'

'Jeans, I guess we should finish our coffee and move ahead.'

'If you are not all right then we can leave, Sands.'

'Now I want to see this place. I want to see what else you can show me here.'

'You're sounding as if you have taken everything personally.'

'I have not taken anything personally, Jeans.'

'Okay, if you really want to see other sections then its fine with me.'

'I am done with my coffee and if you are done then let's go to other sections.'

'Sure, let's go to the terrorist and prison section.'

'Okay.'

'Leave not Inn Zalimoe koe.'

'Is that the name of the section?'

'Yes.'

'Okay.'

'The name of this section is kept after the name of the place where the terrorists are imprisoned. Leave not Inn Zalimoe koe is located in an island called Gapediaeriie which is at deep south west of AlphaLand. The island is guarded 24/7 and 365 days in a year with robust security systems and mechanisms. It takes 50 kilometres from Kubaoratyae island to reach Gapediaeriie. Only defense helicopters, planes, and ships are allowed to go there. All the terrorists and people who are involved in helping the terrorism activities are imprisoned there and no one is allowed to meet them.'

'Okay.'

'Sands, no prisoner till now came out of that place. It is said that once a person goes there then only his/her dead body come out of that place.'

'What?'

'Be it anyone. Once that guy is caught then he or she is just gone. That person will not have even a single chance to escape.'

'Okay.'

'In this section you can see updates on number of terrorists imprisoned, the terrorist organization they were involved into and the type of sentence they are serving. Details about banned organisations and other details are also available.'

'Okay.'

'Sands, if you have any questions then you can ask the representative sitting over here.'

'No, it's okay, I don't have any.'

'Okay, then let's go to the other section.'

'What's next?'

'Defense section.'

'Okay.'

'It is called Hummaraeae Veeroae.'

'Okay.'

'There are various subsections in Hummaraeae Veeroae.'

'Okay.'

'Come, let's get down, we have reached.'

'Okay.'

'As I have told there are various sub sections, like you can see one with sea theme that is Defense Nadeyo section.'

'Okay.'

'Details of various sea routes, rivers, canals, and other water resources on which AlphaLand has control are available. Details of various warships, vessels, submarines, missiles, weapons, bombs, ammunitions, technologies, and other things that are used in sea defense in AlphaLand are available here.'

'Okay.'

'Details of AlphaLand's tie up with other countries are available. You can also see here the list of the great people who worked in the past and who are currently working in the sea defense. In a nut shell all the details about the sea defense are available there.'

'Okay.'

'You can see we have 100 state-of-the-art world class warships and they cost billions. There are water guards and they are alert 24/7 round the clock. AlphaLand is surrounded with so many water bodies so to safeguard of these bodies from any infiltration, the role of water guards become very important.'

'How do these water guards do their job?'

'See, the water guards themselves watch and other than that there are radar systems that read any vessel, boat, or anyone trying to enter AlphaLand. Radar systems give instant alert signal if they find anything suspicious and make the defense people alert.'

'Okay.'

'So what are the various defense categories?'

'For Land we have Defense Bhumiyoae, Air we have Defense Vayoae, for Cyber we have Defense Cyboae, and Underground defense service we have Defense Under Bhumyoae.'

'Okay.'

'Look at the brown colour theme, that's Defense Bhumiyoae.'

'Okay.'

'Here the details regarding the Control of Territory, Defense Equipment, Nuclear Missiles, Technology and other things related to land defense are available.'

'Okay.'

'Sands, the equipment, missiles, tankers, and the other tools used are the best in the world.'

'Okay.'

'Sands, this is Defense Vayoae and its theme is aircrafts. Here the details of the Control of Air Territory, Aircrafts, Radars, Technologies, defense strength, other tools and resources used are available.'

'Okay.'

'You can see the themes for Defense Cyboae, all its computers and technologies and for Defense Under Bhumyoae the theme is tunnels.'

'Okay.'

'Sands, cybercrime and terrorism activity has become quite vibrant in recent times. To counter this, Defense Cyboae works day in and day out. The people working in this are the best minds in the world. They create programs of such a kind that it becomes very difficult for terrorists to infiltrate. In case they are infiltrated, then these guys destroy the infiltration activity within a fraction of seconds.'

'Okay.'

'Sands, they work on very modern and world class technologies. Defense Cyboae also shares very important information with other defense groups and security bodies. This helps to counter terrorism and crime.'

'Okay.'

'In Defense Under Bhumyoae the details about the underground territory control that AlphaLand has are available. In recent times, AlphaLand has made underground tunnels that can help to combat wars. With the help of these tunnels one can reach at critical locations in very less time. This becomes important because many neighbouring countries are trying to expand their defense reach and to counter any future attacks from them these tunnels become crucial.'

'Okay.'

'In Defense Under Bhumyoae details of defense strength, technologies, equipment, arms, vehicles, and other related details are available.'

'Okay.'

'Sands, our five defense systems are the best in the world. The technologies, methodologies, weapons, missiles, antimissiles, bombs, guns, aircrafts, tankers, rockets, nuclear missiles, radar systems, warships, plane or aircraft carriers, defense strength, and any other tools and resources used are the best in the world.'

'Okay.'

'Sands, no one has the courage to challenge and fight our strong and robust defense system. If anybody, by mistake, tries to do it then only heaven knows what repercussions and aftermaths they have to face and bear.'

'Okay.'

'We believe in peace and harmony and that is the reason why we don't wish and neither have intentions to attack anyone. But if anyone dares to attack us, then we don't spare them.'

'Okay.'

'All the technologies, equipment, ships, aircrafts, I mean everything that is used in defense are made in AlphaLand. Lots of investments are done on research and developments and we have world class R&D centres, ordinance factories, and manufacturing centres.'

'Okay.'

'We not only make equipment for ourselves but also export to other countries. We have tie ups with other countries for knowledge sharing.

'Okay.'

'Any questions if you have then you can ask to the representatives or shall we go to other section?'

'Let's move.'

'Well then, let's go to the Economy section.'

'Okay.'

'Arthosastraeyoae.'

'So how does the economy of AlphaLand stand?'

'We will see the details in the section, have some patience.'

'Hmmm.'

'So how many more sections left now?'

'Not many.'

'Okay.'

'We have reached the Economy section.'

'Okay.'

'The Economy section is called Arthosastraeyoae. The Bank of Planetoae which is the world's biggest and powerful bank headquartered in Endraepristae has announced that the economy of AlphaLand is worth fifty thousand trillion Grandaes.'

'I just can't believe this!'

'You have to and it's way ahead of the world's second best economy.'

'What are you saying?'

'AlphaLand constitutes of 70 per cent of the world's economy. In terms of Purchasing Power Parity it is number one in the world and it's number one developed economy in the world with GDP growth rate of 15 per cent.'

'What?'

'The other developed economies of the world don't grow at 15 per cent but it is not the case with AlphaLand.

'It's hard to believe.'

'The agriculture sector contributes 37 per cent; service sector makes up to 34 per cent; and industrial sector contributes to 29 per cent of GDP. Thus this makes AlphaLand an agriculture-based country.'

'I guess I know that.'

'As AlphaLand is an agro-based nation, so special emphasis is given to agriculture. Like the farmers get frequent trainings on the types of crops, fertilizers, and tools. They are trained about seasonal trends and their conduciveness.'

'Okay.'

'Farmers are provided loans at cheaper rates from the banks and they can repay on easy terms. The government also takes special care for education of their children. Their children can avail education through a special plan from the government.'

'Okay.'

'Adulteration is strictly prohibited in AlphaLand. All the fertilizers and tools used for agriculture are of number one quality. They are made in AlphaLand and are of world's best standard.'

'Okay.'

'All the rating agencies of the world rate AlphaLand as a very stable economy with strong fundamentals. They rate AlphaLand as an economy that can survive in any recession and downtime.'

'Okay.'

'Till now no recession has affected AlphaLand and neither shall it affect in the future. Nobody in AlphaLand lost a job because of recession.'

'Okay.'

'Here other details of the various companies, research and development centres and other financial bodies present in AlphaLand are available. Countrywise exports and imports done by AlphaLand are also available.'

'Okay.'

'Any questions, Sands?'

'Well I don't have any, let's move ahead.'

'Okies, let's go to food, health, fitness, cleanliness, and environment section.'

'Okay.'

'Anyae, Tandorustae safayae vatavarnae.'

'What does the name represent?'

'Well Anyae is for food, Tandorustae is for health, Safayae is for cleanliness, and Vatavarnae is for environment.'

'Okay.'

'The names have indigenous touch.'

'Okay.'

'So here we are . . .'

'Yeah.'

'Sands, this section is more about the health clubs, fitness centres, and healthy food joint.'

'Okay.'

'In AlphaLand a lot of emphasis is given to health and fitness. People here believe that health is everything and if one is having a good health then he or she can achieve anything.'

'Okay.'

'Government conducts lots of workshops and training sessions about health and cleanliness across AlphaLand throughout the year. People are educated about the benefits of having good food and they are also told about various types of diets that can be taken for maintaining good health.'

'Okay.'

'People are educated about various types of exercises and yogas that they should do on a daily basis to stay fit. There are various government run food joints, fitness centres, and training centres across AlphaLand.'

'Okay.'

'Many people do exercise at home and follow a strict diet for staying fit. Sands, there is no adulterate food sold in AlphaLand and if anyone found selling it then the license is cancelled, hefty penalty is charged, and that person is given rigorous imprisonment.'

'Okay.'

'The average life expectancy in AlphaLand is 105 years.'

'Are you sure?'

'Of course, yes.'

'Tough to believe. No other country has this much high life expectancy.'

'This is AlphaLand and it is very different from other countries.'

'Still tough to believe. Anyways, let's proceed further.'

'Cleanliness is also given a lot of importance in AlphaLand. People are educated about keeping themselves clean and maintaining cleanliness at home and surroundings. Government's priority is to maintain AlphaLand clean and a pollution-free country.'

'Okay.'

'The roads and other public areas in AlphaLand are washed every day and recycled water generated through waste water is used for this purpose.'

'Okay.'

'In AlphaLand more emphasis is given on the usage of less personal vehicles and more of public transport. Whosoever is the person whether a billionaire or a common man he or she has to use more of public transport. The people should at least use public transport four days a week and this is made mandate from the government.'

'Okay.'

'People are asked to use pollution-free vehicles. They are advised to use more of cycles and hybrid vehicles which are environment-friendly.'

'Okay.'

'It's mandatory that all the vehicles shall go for pollution checks once in three months and any vehicle older than seven years is not allowed to use. After seven years they can be sold to government companies at a decent price and these vehicles are used to make other things by these companies.'

'They are used to make what?'

'Basically, they are used to make industrial tools and any other stuff depending upon their durability and quality.'

'Okay.'

'Here you can check the details like locations of environment centres, food clubs, agencies, fitness centres, etcetera.'

'Okay.'

'Any questions?'

'No questions.'

'Okay, let's move to the Sports Section.'

'Okay.'

'Kridae.'

'So what exactly is there in the sports section?'

'Sands, in this section the details of various types of sports, sports bodies, sports heads, region or zonewise sports details, stadiums, sport centres, race tracks, sportsmen and the medals they have won and so on and so forth are available.'

'Okay.

Sports are very much liked in AlphaLand.'

'Hmmm.'

'So here we are at the sports section.'

'Okay.'

'The sole motto is to win whatever sports we play. There are world's best sports training centres, camps, grounds, tools, technologies, and other facilities available in AlphaLand.'

'Okay.'

'Rigorous selection processes are followed for selecting the best sportsmen. Notifications of the selection are given in various channels, newspapers, and other publications.'

'Okay.'

'Various locations are mapped and the prospective sportsmen are called there for the trials. After the first round, the selected people are called for other rounds of selection. In total there are four rounds of trials and one round for group discussion and personal interview.'

'Why is a group discussion and personal interview conducted? Is it some job selection or what?'

'Sands, GD is done to test how much the candidate is aware about the sports, its policies and procedures and an interview actually gives an opportunity to see why the person wants to join the sports.'

'Okay.'

'It shows whether the person wants to join because of his passion or is it out of some compulsion. It is always advocated that people should join sports if they have passion for it and not by any force or compulsion.'

'Okay.'

'Sands, lots of awareness programs are done to encourage and motivate people to join sports. Sports icons visit to different places to give motivational speeches and they conduct lots of training sessions and workshops for the aspiring sportsmen.'

'Okay.'

'Sands, our national game is Warm Water football but that doesn't mean that we are good only in our national game. We are the best in whatever sports we play and our only aim is to win.'

'Okay.'

'We have been world champs in all events and championships for last ten years and beating us is almost impossible.'

'Jeans, how is Warm Water football played?'

'Well, it's an interesting sport. The ground in which it is played is like a huge pit with cement flooring and cement boundaries. The plastic material is fixed on cement surface and tiles and over them a spongy material is fixed. The ground has a width of forty-five feet, length of sixty feet and depth of five feet.'

'Okay.'

'The cement, tiles, and plastic floorings are fixed from the bottom up to half a feet, of which cement flooring and tiles are of four centimetres thick and the rest are plastic materials. The quality of the plastic material is of such type that it eliminates injuries. The spongy flooring is fixed up to next four and a half feet. The ground is completely filled with warm water and then football is played.'

'Okay.'

'Very few countries play this, but we play this for fun, enjoyment, and good feeling.'

'Okay.'

'Sands, sports are taken quite seriously in AphaLand and per year lots of investments are done by the government in sports.'

'Okay.'

'Any questions if you have then you can ask the representative?'

'No. Let's move to next section.'

'Okay, let's move to Politics section.'

'Okay.'

'Rajnityae.'

'So how many more sections left?'

'Only few are left now.'

'You have been telling this for quite a sometime now.'

'But you said you are ready to see all the section today, right?'

'Yeah, I know.'

'So here is the Politics section.'

'Okay.'

'AlphaLand is one of the world's most populous democratic nations. It has eight recognised national parties and more than thirty-five regional parties.'

'Okay.'

'AlphaLand Party and Alpha Land People's Party are the major parties. They are known for their reforms, vision, and liberal thoughts.'

'Okay.'

'In the Republic of AlphaLand the first general elections were held in 1940 and Mr Hawarae fal was elected as the first Numero One minister of AlphaLand. In this section the details of political history of AlphaLand, various political parties of AlphaLand, Numero One ministers, Cabinate ministers, State ministers, and bureaucrats are available.'

'Okay.'

'The Numero One minister is the most powerful person of AlphaLand and one can say that he or she is the whole and sole of the government.'

'Okay.'

'There are two parliaments in Alphaland which is Badae Niwasae and Chottae Niwasae and all the elected members attend the sessions at these houses.'

'Okay.'

'If you have any questions then you can ask the representative.'

'Nothing much.'

'Okay, then let's go to other section.'

'What is the next section?'

'The section that we are going now is my favorite section.'

'Okay.'

'Let's go to Hummae se uppaerae Kuann.'

'What is this section about?'

'We will find it soon.'

'I hope it shall be interesting.'

'You will have a very amazing experience and that's for sure.'

'Let's see . . .'

'So here it is.'

'What it is all about?'

'Here there are comparison details of AlphaLand with other countries.'

'What?'

'Yes, comparison on various categories like employment, education, defense, technology, and so on and so forth.'

'How authentic is this comparison?'

'It's 100 per cent true as the details are taken from respective world organizations who track the details of each and every country.'

'Okay.'

'Let's starts with education, literacy, and employment. As seen earlier we have 100 per cent literacy rate and 100 per cent employment. In these categories we stand number one in the world.'

'Are you sure?'

'What do you mean by that?'

'Well, nothing.'

'I guess I have already shown you the details in the respective sections.'

'I was just asking, that's it.'

'Let's move further. In crime and terrorism we have 100 per cent control and no other country in the world has this kind of record.'

'I hope this is not exaggerated?'

'What makes you think like that?'

'Because no country in the world has this type of control.'

'But this is true and that's why this is such a great nation.'

'Hard to believe.'

'This is true, Sands. Don't create your own theories, okay?'

'Ah, carry on, please.'

'Yes, I will and please don't ask sarcastic questions, okay?'

'Can we proceed?'

'The way you ask the questions really offends.'

'Well, I don't ask things to offend you.'

'Let's move further. The law and order, judiciary, governance, banking systems of AlphaLand are the best in the world.'

'Hmmm.'

'Any questions if you have?'

'No questions.'

'Our defense systems are the best in the world.'

'Okay.'

'The male to female ratio of AlphaLand is the best in the world, and there is no gender and racial discriminations. We are number one in the world in controlling gender discrimination.'

'Okay.'

'There are no farmer suicide, child labour, female feticide, woman harassment, rape, caste discrimination, and racial discrimination cases in AlphaLand.'

'I just can't believe this!'

'You have to believe this as this is true.'

'I hope these are not fabricated.'

'No, these are not fabricated. Can I proceed?'

'As you wish.'

'All the locations of AlphaLand are most desirable locations in the world for business and investment purposes because of the favorable conditions.'

'Okay.'

'The GDP of AlphaLand is number one in the world. The industries, technologies, research and development centres of AlphaLand are the best in the world.'

'Okay.'

'AlphaLand has great contribution in innovations and inventions in the field of science, technology, engineering, automobiles, aeronautics, aviation, and so on and so forth. Our country's name is always taken with great respect and we are looked upon as a role model by many countries.'

'Okay.'

'Any questions, Sands?'

'No.'

'Sands, the per capita income of AlphaLand is best in the world. You know, Sands, no one in AlphaLand has heard of poverty. No one is poor here, my buddy, no one.'

'I hope you are right.'

'All the politicians of AlphaLand are very well respected around the world. They are known for their vision, communal and social harmony, bonding and selflessness. They are all Great Champs. Sands, this nation is a corrupt-free nation and no other nation has this record. In a nutshell, this is a great land and a blessing to the world.'

'That is not true.'

'You have started again.'

'AlphaLand is not what you are telling me.'

'Sands, have you gone insane?'

'Jeans, this is the height of lies.'

'What lies? How much do you know about AlphaLand?'

'Me knowing about AlphaLand, do you know what you are talking, Jeans? I belong to AlphaLand, it's my country. I know about this place more than anybody else knows.'

'Sands, you have gone nuts. You don't even know what you are talking about.'

'I very much know what I am talking about. AlphaLand is not what you are trying to say, whatever you have said is farcical. The truth is something else. Face the truth and come out of your illusions.'

'What illusions? You have lost your mind, Sands. I thought you are wise and prudent but I am sorry, I have to change my mind now.'

'I don't care what you think about me. The truth doesn't change with your thinking. Whatever you have said looks like some fairytale, so unreal, and flimsy.'

'Sands, you are saying I don't know about AlphaLand and whatever I have said is all flimsy and crap. Then why don't you tell me about AlphaLand as you yourself are proclaiming that you belong to this nation. I would be more than curious to know your version.'

'Jeans, that fact is always bitter and you should have a big heart to accept the truth as all your illusions shall be broken by listening to the fact.'

'Sands, I know you have nothing to say. You are jealous about us and about our great nation because you are not like us. You are not as developed as we are and you don't belong to the number one nation of the world.'

'Why would I be jealous about my own country?'

'From your attitude, it shows how much grudges you are having for us. We have treated you like our guest, I have shown you so many places and this is how you are treating me and my nation.'

'First of all, let me make it clear to you once again that I belong to AlphaLand and I don't have any hatred for my motherland but that doesn't mean that I shall sit blind on the reality. Let me tell you the fact and you listen to it very carefully. AlphaLand is not what you are saying, in AlphaLand our leaders and politicians are not worried about education, literacy, and employment rather they are only worried about money. It doesn't matter to them at all whether someone is illiterate or unemployed in fact they are happy about it so that they can demand more money from the people for providing education and jobs. All these politicians at AlphaLand are just thugs and there is no single party in AlphaLand that is not corrupt. Here, people have only one choice that is to select between bad and worst as all the parties are one and the same in their values and ethics.'

'What the crap you are talking about? I don't know how to react to your sheer ignorance.'

'There is nothing called research and development here. In AlphaLand, young minds are not encouraged to do something new or something innovative. They are taught to follow old routines and do what their elders have done.'

'Sands, just stop it. Don't give me crap.'

'There is no day in AlphaLand that goes without news of scams, scandals, and crime. If any day goes without any of these incidents, then the people of AlphaLand get a feel of shock and they literally pinch themselves to realise whether they are residing in AlphaLand or in some other country. We are soft targets for the terrorists, they come and attack whenever they feel like and we don't do anything. Such is our intelligence and security systems that it takes years to crack a single case.'

'Can you stop now?'

'Massive expenditure is made on defense and to make robust security systems but do you know the amount of corruption involved in that? It's enormous. Corruption is at rampant in AlphaLand and the biggest culprits are the leaders, politicians, and a lot of other big and powerful guys. Fair selection in education, employment, governance, administration, civil services, and be it any other field has gone for a toss long time back. Only one thing that prevails is corruption, crime, scams, nepotism, and favoritism.'

'Enough now?'

'The poor starve to death without food and other facilities, but our so called leaders, politicians, and bureaucrats don't even care. They are just busy in making money for themselves. If any case gets filed in AlphaLand especially by a common man against some powerful person then it goes on for years and years without any results. Everyone knows that the powerful chap is the culprit but still he or she roams freely. Nothing happens to that person and the poor dies while fighting the case against him. This is how our beloved nation is. For the namesake we are a democratic country but in reality, if anyone tries to express his or her thought, then no one knows what that person has to pay for it especially when that person speaks the truth.'

'Will you zip your mouth or else I will leave right now!'

'You are talking about harassment done on women, female feticides, and child abuse. Jeans, it happens every day in AlphaLand. There is nothing called evenness, fairness, and justice in this nation and Laws and Rules are made by those people who have power and might.'

'Sands, one word from you and I will leave.'

'The common man keeps on paying taxes but no one cares where his or her hard earned money has gone. It goes into the pockets of our beloved politicians. Jeans, this is not the world's number one nation rather it is the world's one of the most corrupt and hypocrite nations.'

'Sands, I thought you are a nice man who is gentle, kind, understanding, and wise. I treated you like a friend and tried to give you the hospitality that is given to a guest in AlphaLand. But I was so wrong. You are a sick guy and you don't deserve any hospitality and friends. Bye, Sands, and thanks for treating me and my country so badly. I shall never forgive you for this.'

'Jeans, wait, where are you going?'

'Bye, Sands.'

'Please don't go like this.'

'You have made fun of my nation.'

'Wait! Wait, Jeans! Wait!'

'If such are your thoughts about AlphaLand then what makes you stay in AlphaLand?'

'My hopes and dreams, Jeans. They tell me every day that one day things shall change for the better. I want to see that change, I want to make that change and I want to thrive for it. I have a belief that one day AlphaLand shall become like what you have said and shown. I know it shall take some time but, Jeans, you don't know my countrymen, they will not give up. We all will stand together and make this nation a true gold. Jeena, Jeena, wait.'

'Bye, Sands.'

Chapter Seven

Waking up from the Dream

'Please, please don't go. I didn't want to hurt you. Jeena! *Aahhhh!* What is this? Who the hell is this? *Aaah!* My ears, leave it please! *Aah!* My ears are gone. Who the hell is it?'

'You idiot! What were you speaking and who is Jeans?'

'Oh, Mom! When have you come and what are you doing here?'

'You are dreaming about girls, is this the age for this? What's wrong with you, Sandeep? Tell me, who is this girl?'

'Mom, there is no such girl. It's just a dream, trust me, please.'

'The sad part is you get these kinds of dreams. It's high time to concentrate on your studies as your exams are not very far and I don't want you to do badly in your twelfth exams. Your dad and I, want you to top your twelfth exams and after that we want you to pursue your career in engineering. Is this how you are going to top the exams?'

'Mom, I am studying hard.'

'It's high time. Better concentrate hard on your studies and I don't want you to have this kind of dreams.'

'Okay, Mom.'

'Tell me one thing.'

'Yes, Mom?

'Are you in love with anyone?'

'No, Mom, why are you asking questions like that?'

'Better stay away from all these crap. Now get ready for you classes or else you shall be late.'

'Yes, Mom.'

'I have kept milk and vegetable sandwich on the table, have it before leaving.'

'Sure, Mom.'

'I am going to Pamila auty's house okay. Lock the door properly before leaving.'

'Bye, Mom, see you later.'

'Bye.'

*****

'Hey, hey, hey, where are you going? Friends, I know my dream is a little different but one thing is common that we all want the kind of AlphaLand that has been shown by Jeans and for that we need to work harder like Mom has said I need to work harder to clear my twelfth. Friends, I know it's not easy but we have to and as wise people say "charity begins at home" so we need to first introspect ourselves and first try to change ourselves for the better. Instead of blaming others on what they have done we need to see what we have done and what could have been done better and only then we can change as a nation. Friends, we have to put faith on ourselves and hope that one day we shall make our nation as world's best nation. We have to make a change for our better future, coming generation's better future and our nation's better future. Friends, we have to give all that we can to make AlphaLand the world's best nation. Cheers! *Oopps!* I am getting late, Mom will kill me but guys, let's make AlphaLand an Eldorado.'

My Country

Everybody says it's my country
But how many realises their duty
Every day we see crime
But are afraid to do anything at that time

The poor dies of hunger
The orphan dies without shelter
The women are confused to decide
Whether it is safe to go outside

Everywhere there is frustration
Law and order has no solution
Passing the buck has become daily routine
And everyone wants to show that they are clean

The time has come to take some action
If we really feel that it's our nation
Otherwise everything shall go haywire
And we shall never come out of this barbed wire

Let's help the deprived and poor
Let's make the underprivileged come out of fear
Let's remove illiteracy from the country
And spreading education shall become everyone's
    responsibility

Let's eradicate the cases of female feticide
Let's give faith to women that they are safe outside
Let the old live with dignity
Let the newborn see prosperity

Let's take a vow that there shall be no caste and creed
    distance
Let everyone has fair chance of existence
Let's remove the situation of unemployment
Let everyone has satisfaction and fulfilment

Let's not blame anyone for failures
Let's take collective measures
Let's make our nation strong
As this is where we actually belong

Synopsis

He comes to an Alien Land where everything is like a fairytale. Everything is so perfect that it can be seen only in dreams and highly impossible to happen in reality. He finds that the place where he went to has the same name as his own country. How is Sandeep going to accept this? Is he going to agree to whatever he has seen or is he just going to deny and consider all that he has seen is just an illusion? How will Jeena react to Sandeep's arguments? Will they remain friends or will they part ways and never be in touch with each other? A very different and eye opening experience where the journey of Sandeep in AlphaLand is not that easy as it has lots of twists and turns, denials, arguments, and fights, and comparisons with hard reality.

This book shows a dream which is seen by a common man each and every day, where there is no surety whether whatever is dreamt can be real but there are hopes that one day, things shall change for the better and dreams may come true.